Vam... Killer

EMILY SHADOWHUNTER
BOOK ONE

CRAIG ZERF

Vampire Killer (Emily Shadowhunter, Book One) © 2018 by Craig Zerf

As always – to my wife, Polly and my son, Axel. You chase the shadows from my soul.

Chapter 1

It was not the first time Emily had flown. In fact, it was not even the first time she had flown First Class. Not that she was from a super-privileged background or anything. Well, she probably was, way back when. She had lived in a Malibu mansion and her parents had been a couple of real international jet setter types.

So, Emily had done a lot of traveling. Not so much with her parents but with her rich friends and, most often, with paid companions. Ski instructors, diving instructors. Even flying instructors.

That had all stopped when her parents died. When she was eleven years old.

Her mom and dad had never spent much face time with her. She used to think that was because they simply weren't cut out to be hands-on parent types. They were high-flyers and international-party-goers, as opposed to bedtime storytellers and school-play watchers.

She had been wrong. There had been nothing they had wanted more than to tuck her in at night and read her stories about bears that go shopping. Or have family takeout night, eat pizza and rent bad horror movies.

But while some parents are allowed that freedom, others are tied to a higher, selfless purpose.

After their deaths, Emily had been taken in by a pair of family friends. She had known them the whole of her short life and, whilst she did not see them often, she liked them both and was happy to go with them.

Not that there was any choice.

'Excuse me, ma'am,' the air hostess interrupted her reverie. 'We're about to take off. Please could you fasten your seat belt and put your chair in the upright position.'

Emily nodded, smiled, complied, and then let her mind slip back into the past.

They had never officially fostered

Emily and she had never thought of them as mom and dad. But she had felt close to them. As close as they had allowed her to feel, as they often came across more as tutors than as family.

Bartholomew and Ryoko Johnson. Both were in their mid-forties. Ryoko had been born in Japan. She was small, neat, and quiet. He was the polar opposite. A big man, in both voice and stature. Long unkempt hair and beard, bright, deep-blue eyes. Muscles like burlap bags stuffed with eels.

The biggest shock was that she had been moved to Alaska. A pampered Malibu princess, torn from her mild and sunny comfort zone to a state often referred to as 'The Last Frontier'. The wild land mass where the population density was less than one person per square mile and the temperature was known to drop to minus twenty-eight degrees.

The reason Bart and Ryoko lived in Alaska was because they were both rabid 'Preppers'. They preferred to call themselves 'Survivalists' but it came down to the same thing – they were thoroughly prepared for the Big One. Whether that took place as a nuclear holocaust, a worldwide viral outbreak or an alien invasion, a good Prepper was ready for anything. With a stout underground bunker, enough dried food and water for two years survival, an armory capable of supplying a full-scale private war, and all of the necessary skills – Bart and Ryoko were at the top of the game.

When Emily had asked Bartholomew what he thought was going to go wrong, he laughed out loud and replied – 'Darling, don't you know? It's already happened.'

She hadn't bothered to ask him again.

'Champagne or freshly squeezed orange juice?' asked the hostess, dragging Emily once more from her cogitation.

Emily thought a bit before she answered. Technically, the American liquor laws stated that she was still underage. But then she was going to England and apparently the legal age for drink there was eighteen. So, after a few seconds of internal debate she decided she had better get some practice in before she arrived.

'Champagne, please.'

The golden drink cascaded into her crystal flute, the bubbles rising and spinning, picking up the white of the overhead cabin lights as it did so.

She took a sip. The effervescence tickled her nose. It was tart and sweet at the same time. Like grape soda that had gone off. She shrugged, took another sip, decided it was a bit meh and put it down.

When she had first arrived in Alaska she had made the mistake of thinking of Bart and Ryoko as country hicks. Good solid people who loved the flag, guns, and apple pie in equal measure. It didn't take her long to discover her mistake.

Bart was actually a professor of philosophy from New York University, he was also an ex-marine and a weapons and tracking expert.

Ryoko, who had been born in Hinohara outside Tokyo, Japan, was a third dan black belt in Kung Fu and Jiu Jitsu, as well as a being a graduate of Cal Tech in applied mathematics. The Japanese woman was almost the diametric opposite of Emily who was tall, blonde, blue-eyed and just curvy enough to attract attention. Ryoko was tiny, dark haired, serious, and thin to the point of androgyny.

Due to the remoteness of the area, Emily had been home schooled by her two foster parents and, as such, had achieved a postgraduate level of education in both mathematics and philosophy by the time she was seventeen. She had also achieved her second-level black belt in Kung Fu and her first dan in Jiu Jitsu. She could achieve minute-of-angle shooting with a rifle and was a qualified Master Rank with a handgun. She could track a variety of animals through any weather and terrain, live off the land, speak both Latin and ancient Greek and bake a perfect cheese soufflé nine times out of ten.

However, she was guilty of biting her nails and tended to stand with a bit of a stoop, almost as if she were embarrassed at her slightly above average height.

But then she never claimed to be perfect. In fact, Emily never claimed to be anything. She had no yardstick against which to measure herself. And her infrequent visits to Anchorage did not allow her any time for either socializing or comparing herself to others.

In fact, Emily would have considered herself to be pretty normal.

Until she turned eighteen. Only yesterday.

Already it seemed so long ago...

...*Bart woke her even earlier than was usual in the Johnson household.* A knock on the door, a cup of coffee, a brisk Happy Birthday darling and a request to join him and Ryoko in the kitchen as soon as she was ready.

She showered and changed into her usual two-piece black kung fu suit and canvas shoes. Comfortable, practical clothing. Neither Ryoko nor Bart believed in frivolous fashion and, truth be told, Emily did hanker after a wardrobe full of girly clothes. Designer outfits, branded jeans and shoes worn for looks rather than practicality.

She walked into the kitchen and both of her foster parents where there, waiting for her. Bart gave her a hug and then Ryoko did the same, but she held on to Emily for a good minute, which was unusual as she wasn't normally a demonstrative person at all.

Finally, she stood back and handed Emily a small box that she had tied with a ribbon. Emily opened it to reveal a silver necklace. The chain made up of three delicate strands that had been plaited together. Hanging from it, a carved Japanese symbol in jade. She slid it over her head.

'It's beautiful,' she said appreciatively. 'Thank you.'

Ryoko smiled at her. 'It has been in our family for over one thousand years. Passed down from mother to daughter in an unbroken line.'

Emily held up the jade symbol. 'What does this say?'

'It is hard to translate into the western tongue,' the small Japanese woman answered. 'But if one had to try, I suppose one could say – "The Brightest

Flame Casts the Deepest Shadow". It is all about Ying and Yang. Those of us who are capable of the best of deeds are also capable of the darkest. It is both a message of warning and an amulet of protection against the darkness. Wear it always.'

'I will,' responded Emily.

'Right, my girl,' interjected Bart. 'Look, there's something we have to tell you.' He looked pensive when he spoke. Unsure of himself. Which was an expression Emily had never seen before on the big man's face. There was a long awkward silence and then eventually he said.

'You know what; it's easier to simply show you. Come on, let's go to the dojo.'

The three of them traipsed through the house and into the dojo, a large open room with sprung wooden floors and a series of punch bags and *makiwara* punching boards along the one wall.

Bart grabbed two blocks of wood and laid them down next to each other, then he placed a concrete roof tile across them.

Emily knew what that was for. She had practiced her knife-hand strike until she was capable of breaking a roof tile with her bare hand. Once she had managed to break two. Only once.

But Bart continued to pile more tiles on. Two. Three. Four, five. Ten.

Then he stopped.

'Break them,' he instructed.

Emily shook her head. 'No way.'

'Way,' urged Bart. 'Trust me, my girl. You can do it.'

Emily glanced at Ryoko for support, but the petite Asian woman simply nodded her agreement and pointed at the vast mountain of tiles. 'You can do it,' she repeated. 'See it happening. Envisage it. And then make it happen.'

Emily didn't want to disappoint her foster parents, so she stepped forward, stood in front of the ludicrously high pile of concrete, composed herself and struck.

The tiles simply exploded. Each one broke into at least five pieces.

Emily squealed in shock and jumped backwards like she had been bitten.

Both Bart and Ryoko smiled.

But their smiles were tinged with another expression. Acceptance. And perhaps sadness.

Emily didn't notice, such was her shock at what she had just achieved.

'Umm...there's more,' said Bart, almost apologetically. 'Come,' he led Emily to the window. 'Can you see that? Nailed to the tree over there on the horizon.' He pointed at an letter paper sized piece of paper, nailed to a tree some one thousand and seventy-two yards away. Bart knew the exact distance because he had paced it out that morning.

Emily nodded. 'Yep. Just.'

'How far away is it?'

Emily shrugged. 'About half a mile.'

'No. Exactly how far?'

The teenage girl concentrated. 'One thousand and seventy-two yards and four inches...damn. How did I do that?'

Again, Bart and Ryoko smiled. 'Read what it says,' said Ryoko.

'Oh, come on. Really?'

Ryoko nodded.

Again, Emily stared and concentrated, squinting her eyes up in an attempt to focus.

'Don't squint,' said Bart. 'No need. Trust me.'

'Okay,' said Emily. 'It says, name Pi to as many decimal places as you can.'

As an accomplished mathematician Emily knew Pi was a mathematical constant. It was the ratio of a circles circumference to its radius. It is also known as an irrational number, meaning that it is infinite.

She started to reel off the numbers.

'

3.14159265358979323846264338327950288419716939937510...'

'Enough,' said Bart. 'Could you do that yesterday?'

'You know I couldn't. What the hell has happened to me?' asked Emily, her voice verging on panic.

'Come on,' said Bart softly. 'Let's go back to the kitchen, get some breakfast. There's a lot we need to talk about.'

And then, over pancakes and bacon, Bart and Ryoko changed Emily's life utterly and completely.

'It all started over two thousand years ago, around five hundred BC,' said

Bart. 'When a young Greek man named Ambrogio, traveled to the Delphic Oracle in order to have his fortune told. When he arrived at the temple he saw, and fell in love with, a young priestess named Selene. She returned his feelings. However, Selene was also a favorite of the god Apollo and he was so jealous that, in a fit of rage, he cursed Ambrogio. He decreed the very touch of the sun would burn him and also the slightest feel of silver would bring him unbearable pain. On top of this he also cursed him with immortality so he would be forced to watch his love, Selene, age and die.'

'Whoa,' interjected Emily. 'Harsh much? I mean, give the guy a break, surely Apollo could get any girl he wanted? He must have been like the Chris Hemsworth of his day, why the big deal over Selene?'

Bart raised an eyebrow. 'Who knows how gods think? To the best of my knowledge I have always found them to be both spoiled and capricious beings. Like toddlers with untold power. Best not to offend them. Anyway, Emily, pay attention, this is no fable being told for your amusement, this is a very important.'

'Hold on,' blurted Emily. 'You have always found them? What do you mean?'

But Bart ignored her question and continued. 'After many years, Artemis, the goddess of hunting who was oft an antagonist of Apollo, took pity on Ambrogio as he wandered, both lonely and alone, and so she gifted him with great hunting skills. These included sharp claws, incredible speed, large fangs as well as the ability to shape-shift into other animals at will.

She also gifted him with the knowledge that if he mixed his saliva with another's blood through biting them, he could pass on his immortality and his gifts—although that person would not always be compatible, so they might actually die instead. However, it was too late to save Selene who was already on her death bed due to old age.

Ambrogio became embittered at the loss of his love and stalked the land, killing and changing people at random.

Particularly young women. Over time, he and his house grew very powerful and he spread a reign of terror throughout the land.

The ancient Greeks called Ambrogio and his people, The Shadow People. Or People of the Shades. Nowadays we would call them, Vampires.'

'Vampires?' asked Emily, her disbelief written plainly on her face.

Both Ryoko and Bart nodded in agreement and Emily could see this was no practical joke. They were deadly serious.

'Now,' continued the big man. 'Around 300BC Aristotle and Plato started an academy called The Olympus Foundation. From the very best philosophers and warriors of the time they put together a team to hunt down and destroy these Shadow People and their organizations before they literally usurped mankind. Over the next few centuries this ultra-secret society became more and more of a closed clique as the members were encouraged to marry amongst themselves in order to create a group of super-humans, selectively bred to enhance their inherent and learned powers.

These people are called Shadowhunters. Your parents were both members of this elite group. In fact, they both come from the line of one of the original Shadowhunter couples. An unbroken line that stretches back over two thousand years. And now you have reached your eighteenth birthday, your birthright has manifested. Emily, you are a Shadowhunter.'

The teenager shook her head. It was too much to process. She didn't want to believe it. And, in point of fact, if she hadn't just demonstrably proven something weird had happened to her, she would have simply put her head in the sand and refused to take part.

However, she couldn't deny she could read a typewritten message on a tree over half a mile away. Or that she could now recite Pi to over a thousand places. Or that she had easily reduced a two-foot-high pile of concrete slabs to rubble with a single strike of her bare hand.

But vampires? Shadowhunters? Seriously? Both Ryoko and Bart were staring at her, waiting for a reaction.

'No shit,' she said. 'Do I get some sort of superhero outfit? You know, Spandex body stocking, PVC boots and a polyester cloak.'

Bart laughed. 'Nah, doesn't work like that. Would be cool though.'

Strangely enough, Ryoko smiled but also started to cry at the same time, tears rolled silently down her cheeks. 'There's more,' she said, but she couldn't continue as she buried her head in her hands.

'What's wrong?' Emily asked Bart. 'Why's Ryoko crying?'

'Look, Emily, my darling. We have known this day would arrive but, well, I suppose, whatever you know, you can never adequately prepare for it. You see, Emily, in this world of ours the Shadowhunters are pretty much all that stands between humanity and the darkness. They are what protect us all from the rising of the Shadow. They alone are equipped to fight the vilest of evils. And although that includes vampires it also encompasses much more. Ghouls, demons, black-witches. For evil is legion and we are but few. As such, your life is no longer your own. As from today your major reason for existence is to combat the Shadows. To rid the world of evil. To be a Shadowhunter.'

'So? That doesn't explain why Ryoko is so upset.'

'Emily, now you have come of age and your powers are starting to show, you need to be trained. And we are not qualified to show you what you are capable of. We have done the best we can, but the furthering of your training must now take place elsewhere.'

Emily shook her head. 'No way. What if I don't want to leave?'

Bart smiled. 'Really? You want to live in the asshole of nowhere for the rest of your life. Three hundred miles from the nearest neighbor, with only a bi-annual trip into the city of Anchorage for entertainment?'

'Well, no. I would like to go someplace. See the world. But I also don't want to leave.'

'Can't do both, my sweetheart. Because the only way to get someplace is by leaving someplace else.'

'True,' admitted Emily. 'And exactly where would this someplace else be? And when?'

'Well, the Olympus Foundation world headquarters are currently in London, England,' answered Bart, 'And as for when—' He glanced at his watch.

'Whoa,' interrupted Emily. 'What's with the whole, looking at the watch thing? When I asked I expected you to look for a calendar. What are we talking? Hours or days?'

Bart had the grace to look embarrassed. He shook his head. 'Not hours.'

'So, days then?'

As Emily spoke she heard the dull thump-thump-thump of an approaching helicopter. She jumped up and ran to the window to see a black Bell Jet Ranger cruising in over the tree tops. It flared out at the last moment and landed outside their house, kicking up a vast cloud of snow as it did so.

She turned to Bart. 'Now? You gotta be kidding me.'

'I'm sorry,' said Ryoko. 'We couldn't say anything until your eighteenth birthday. Just in case your powers did not display. The Foundation had agreed, if we didn't contact them then they would be here mid-morning to pick you up. For your own safety. You need to learn how to control your powers.'

'Also,' interjected Bart. 'Now you're a bona fide Shadowhunter, you might find yourself in some danger. It's a big "might", but we didn't want to take a chance.'

Emily didn't know how to react. She was pissed off such a momentous thing had just been sprung on her with no warning. She was also excited she was going to London. Yet, at the same time she was nervous as all hell. And she was upset at the prospect of leaving the only people she had known throughout the last few years.

However, as was her usual habit, she decided to suck it up and simply attack the whole thing head-on.

'Right. I suppose I'd better get packed then.'

Bart grinned. 'That's my girl,' he said proudly.

Emily went back to her bedroom, followed closely by Ryoko…

…And now, after three connecting flights, she was on her way to London, England, and the headquarters of the Olympus Foundation.

Her initial excitement had long since evaporated to be replaced with both trepidation and a not-small dose of genuine fear.

Sometimes life just sucks, she said to herself as the hostess approached and put her meal on her fold down table. Lobster thermidor with French fries and spring vegetables.

Emily smiled to herself. *Yep, sometimes life does suck,* she repeated. *But when you're flying first class then sometimes it sucks just a little bit less.*

Chapter 2

A tall man dressed in a chauffeur's outfit complete with cap, was waiting for Emily when she came out of arrivals. He was holding a sign with her name written on it in beautiful gothic script. Emily Hawk.

She walked up to him, carrying her one and only bag.

'Hi,' she said, holding her hand out. 'I'm Emily.'

He didn't acknowledge her hand or her greeting but simply turned slowly and started to walk towards the exit. Emily shrugged and followed.

Outside, parked in the no stopping zone, was a Rolls Royce Silver Wraith. The chauffeur walked over to it. As they approached a young man got out of the car. Maybe early to mid-twenties.

He was dressed in casual, but ultra-expensive gear. All of it the same shade of midnight black. Gucci Sneakers. Levi vintage jeans, Valentino T-shirt and an Elder Statesmen cashmere hoodie. At least $6000 worth of designer clothing. Emily didn't get out much, but she did have a computer and spent a lot of time online. Vogue, Elle, Iconique. And although she didn't actually remember reading about the man's exact ensemble, she obviously had. Because she knew what each item was, as well as its retail value and where one would shop for the items. It was like her new-found abilities had provided her with instant access to everything she had ever seen or read. *Talk about information overload*, she thought to herself. *I've become a walking version of Google.*

The man scowled at the chauffeur before he spoke, his voice well-modulated but obviously used to command.

'Phineas,' he said. 'Help Miss Emily with her bag, this instant.'

The chauffeur stopped mid stride, turned on his heel, and snatched Emily's holdall from her before continuing to the Rolls and placing it in the trunk.

'Sorry about that,' said the young man. 'He's an adequate driver but his social graces are far from exemplary.'

He walked up to Emily, his hand outstretched in greeting.

Emily took in the rest of him, the person beyond the clothes. Blond hair, cut short on the sides with a bit of length and some volume on the top. Carefully styled to look as if it hadn't been styled at all. A hint of stubble on his chin. Eyes a bright summer-sky blue. Teeth as white as hotel sheets. Maybe two inches taller than her, which put him at five nine or ten. A gymnast's body. Moved with confidence and grace.

For some reason the mere sight of him irritated her. Too much confidence, too much money, and simply...too much.

But he seemed friendly, and Emily wasn't long on friends at the moment, so she took his hand and shook it.

'Emily, I'm so pleased to meet you,' he said enthusiastically as he shook her hand. 'My name's Nathan Tremblay, I believe we're from the same neck of the woods.'

'Umm...Alaska?'

'Well, Canada actually. But practically neighbors.'

Yeah, thought Emily. *Give or take four thousand miles or so.*

Nathan opened the door and ushered her in.

Emily settled into the plush soft-leather seat and stretched her legs out in front of her, marveling at the amount of room in the back of the huge limousine. There was a privacy screen between the passenger seats and the driver, as well as blinds on the windows, reading lights, armrests, and a small bar and refrigerator built into the back of the driver's seat.

Nathan opened the fridge and took out a pack of protein bars. Twelve of them. He offered the pack to Emily.

'Here, I'm sure you're starving. I remember when I first manifested. Body went mental for protein, could have eaten a horse. Don't worry, it stops after a while. Well, actually, it never stops, but it gets better. The insatiable hunger, I mean.'

Emily stared at the box of protein bars and then suddenly realized Nathan was right, she was ravenously hungry. She took out a bar, unwrapped it and took a bite.

'You see,' the young man continued. 'Because you've just turned, your body is adjusting. Over the next few weeks you're going to probably double in weight. Maybe even more.'

Emily flinched 'Eek – what? Good God, I'll be huge. That's awful. I'll need one of those gross cart things people use in Walmart so they can buy their Reece's Pieces and Pop Tarts to keep topping up their obesity problems.'

Nathan laughed. 'No, silly. You'll stay the same size. Perhaps even drop a size. But the density of your muscles will increase as you get stronger and stronger. You see, the denser you get the heavier you are. I mean denser as in mass, not as in Doh! Not sure what you weigh now.'

'One hundred and thirty-two pounds,' blurted Emily.

'Cool, then I would figure on topping out at around three hundred plus in a few weeks' time.'

Emily shuddered. 'I'll be like Baby Huey, grotesque.'

She opened another bar and hoovered it up without even thinking. After a minute or so she looked down in surprise to see the box was empty.

Nathan grinned and handed her another box.

Emily blushed but opened it and got to chewing.

'Where we going?' she asked between bites.

'Pankhurst Manor. It's a huge Victorian pile on the outskirts of London. Mind you, we don't spend as much time there as we used to, mainly we use it for training. There are so few of us now – tend to rattle around in the old place a little. It's not like the old days. I tell you, Emily, those were golden days. The manor was full, honored guests, balls. We were all feted by world leaders, great actors, and the cognoscenti. Great days indeed.'

Emily raised an eyebrow. Nathan was

talking like some old codger, rambling on about the golden days. The expressions didn't sit well coming out of such a young mouth.

She shook her head and slapped her thigh. 'Well, goldarnit. Dem old days was just peachy keen, weren't they?' she chuckled.

Nathan displayed the mere ghost of a smile.

'Oh, come on Nathan,' continued Emily. 'You sound like someone from one of the old timey movies banging on about the glory days. I mean, hell, what are you, twenty-two?'

Nathan nodded. 'Almost right. Just put a one in front of the equation.'

'What, twenty-three?'

He laughed. 'No, actually, I didn't say add a one. I said put in a one in front of the twenty-two.'

Emily paused for a few seconds. 'One hundred and twenty-two?'

'Spot on, Emily. One hundred and twenty-two years old.'

'But that's impossible.'

'A bit of advice, Emily. You're going to have to drop the word, impossible, from your vocabulary for a while. Because you're probably going to see at least two or three impossible things every day from here on in.'

'But one hundred and twenty-two?'

'We age slowly.' Nathan looked her up and down, his expression one of appraisal. 'So,' he said. 'I hope you're relatively happy with the way you look right now, because that's pretty much how you're going to look for the next fifty years or so. If we were allowed to live out our natural lives in peace, then we'd probably check out at around a millennium. A good one thousand years old.'

Emily shook her head. 'Wow,' she exclaimed. 'Imagine the size of the cake you'd need to fit all those candles on.'

She went to grab another protein bar, but the box was finished.

Nathan handed her another one.

Chapter 3

The meeting in the grand hall was almost over. What had needed to be said had been said. Recriminations had been cast where necessary and praise had been given if called for.

But truth be told, there was little call for praise. After all, the fact of the matter was simple – they had still not found what they had been looking for.

And after a thousand years of searching, that was simply not good enough.

It was the first time in almost seventy years Lord Byron Chelsea had been compelled to call a complete meeting of The House. Obviously, he hadn't gone as far as inviting the Familiars or the over one thousand Grinders. The subject to be discussed was simply way too important for them. And anyway, the Grinders' brains were too damaged to comprehend what the meeting was about, and he was confident there would be no real danger, so their presence was unnecessary.

But he had insisted the rest of the three hundred kindred attend.

In the vampire hierarchy there are four basic levels of rank. Level I was a mere Familiar. These are humans who are vampire wanabees. Little more than servants. A mixture of men and women who are either looking for power and immortality, or simply loners looking for a place to belong. Some are just idiotic teenagers who think vamps are cool. Overdosed on a surfeit of Twilight novels to the point they no longer see the fangs and blood-sucking. Only the suaveness, sophistication, and tailored clothes. Basically, idiots. Although they are primarily treated as servants, doing daylight errands like carrying messages, they often simply end up as food. However, sometimes they were rewarded and turned but it is unusual for a vampire to turn anyone without very good reason.

The vampire virus is carried in the

creature's saliva, so, when one decides to turn a prospect, they simply bite them. It matters not if they kill them in the process as, ultimately, the virus will decide their fate. Some will reanimate, and others will either stay dead or die.

The ones that turn do so in one of two ways.

Firstly, they either become level II's. These are lower order vampires.

The virus doesn't kill them, but it burns them. Their brains are badly damaged, and they are left with physical power and speed, longevity, fast healing, but not immortality. They are mere drones with severely impaired mental capacity and a penchant for serious violence.

Most of the humans that are turned become level II's. The full vampires refer to these as Grinders.

Finally, level III's are successfully turned vamps. These are named as Aspirants. They have access to full powers but have not fully grown into them yet. It takes many hundreds of years for a vampire to mature into his or her powers, such as the ability to glamour, or control people's minds.

When they do, they become level IV's or Masters.

Lord Byron was over one thousand years old and was the head of the United Kingdom House. As such he was referred to as a Grand Master.

In the room before him stood seven of his eight Hydra, or lieutenants, as well as another three hundred brethren.

Next to him stood his eighth Hydra and his second in command. Radford Cromwell, the head of the *Nosferatu* Enforcers. The killing arm of the House of Byron. Radford was referred to by all simply as Enforcer and they had done so for the past six hundred years.

Lord Byron cast his eyes over his assembled kindred. 'I have spoken,' he said. 'We must redouble our efforts. Use your familiars to seek during the day. Take yourselves into the darkness every night. We must not rest until it is found. Now go, my children. Go forth and find that which we seek. For our time approaches. The time of the *Nosferatu*. The time of the Shadows.'

Chapter 4

It took over fifteen minutes for the Rolls to travel from the gatehouse to the actual mansion. And when they arrived, the sight took Emily's breath away, and not in a good sense.

The place was like Hogwarts on steroids. It was all towers and flying buttresses and ribbed arches. Intricately mullioned windows sparkled in the wan English sun and literally hundreds of carved grotesques leered down from the roofs and gutters, their faces a panoply of nightmares.

'So,' said Nathan. 'What do you think?'

'It's very…' Emily searched for the right words, not wanting to offend before she'd even taken her first step out of the car.

'It's a massive pile of crap,' said Nathan. 'Looks like every kiddie's nightmare wrapped up into one gigantic, cold, gray heap of stone. Made poorer by the fact that it's no longer full of guests.'

Emily laughed. 'Well, I didn't want to say.'

'Don't worry,' reassured Nathan. 'It's different once you get inside.'

'Oh,' responded Emily.

'Yeah,' continued the old young man. 'It's worse. Anyway, don't let me put you off. Let's go in and meet and greet. Phineas will take care of your luggage.'

She followed Nathan up the stone stairs to the massive front door where he raised the iron knocker and banged it down a couple of times. The noise echoed through the interior and a few seconds later the door creaked open. Inside stood a man in a dark suit and tie. His eyes were blank and his face devoid of any expression.

Emily greeted him, but he didn't react, simply stood still holding the door open.

'Oh, don't worry about him,' said Nathan. 'That's Fergus. I think. Actually, maybe it's Duncan. Whatever, they don't talk much so don't feel like you're being singled out for the silent treatment. Just ignore him. Come on, follow me, I'll introduce you to the boss man.' Nathan walked fast, taking seemingly random corridors and steps. The interior of the mansion was like a maze but, although Emily didn't know where she was in relation to where they were actually heading, she wasn't lost. Her mind automatically tracked every turn, every change of direction and every flight of steps. It felt like she had an internal SatNav monitoring and storing her progress.

'Your bedroom is down there,' said Nathan as he pointed down a corridor. 'Third door on the left. It's quite nice actually, en suite with a great view and a massive fireplace. Got a couple of creepy paintings but nothing that'll keep you awake, I'm sure. I'll take you there after you've met our esteemed leader. We all stay in this wing of the house, nowadays. The other two residential wings are closed on a permanent basis. No need for them anymore.'

As Nathan spoke he stopped outside a

large door, rapped twice, and then opened it and walked in. Emily followed.

The room appeared to be a library. The drapes were drawn shut and a few large church candles wavered in the far reaches of the room. The walls were lined with book filled shelves. The ceiling was so high as to be shrouded in shadow, although it was just possible to see it had been painted with a series of frescos, á la Sistine Chapel. A pair of wheeled ladders leaned against the shelves.

In the center of the room a large desk was covered in piles of papers and opened books. On the right-hand side of the room stood an old man, his back to them as he stared into the fire that burned ferociously in the huge inglenook fireplace. The orange flames provided both warmth as well as most of the light in the room, causing the shadows to dance and flicker about. Shadow puppets without a master.

The man wore a dark, silk robe and his gray hair lay in a thick pony tail that hung down his back to his waist. It was obvious from the breadth of his shoulders and his upright stance that, although old, he was still fit and strong.

'The purpose of knocking, my dear boy,' he sniped, 'is to wait until the resident of the room gives permission to enter. It is not merely some form of warning you are about to barge into a man's inner sanctum.'

'Apologies, Ambros. But I thought you'd like to meet Emily. I picked her up this morning.'

The old man turned to face them, staring intently at Emily as he did so. The first thing the young girl noticed about him was his eyes. Deep purple. Like they had been carved from pure amethyst and then backlit. She shivered slightly as she felt the power behind them and a thrill of real fear ran through her.

Then they suddenly changed, the light dimmed, and the color faded to a light blue. The man smiled, and everything was all right.

He stepped forward, his hand held out in front of him. 'My darling, Emily,' he greeted as he took her hands in his and held them. 'It is an honor and a privilege to have you here with us.'

He stared intently at her for a few seconds and then nodded. 'I can see your father and your mother in you,' he said. 'But you favor your mother's side. Fair of skin and of appearance. Welcome, my child. I am Sir Ambros, the current leader of this little enclave of souls. How are you settling in?'

'Actually, I've just got here,' answered Emily. 'Haven't even seen my room yet.'

'Scandalous,' said Ambros with a grin. 'And I'd bet you're hungry as well.'

Emily nodded. 'Starving,' she admitted.

'That'll be the change,' observed Ambros. 'The kitchen is always open. Tell any of the servants you want food and they will see to it. Try to get at least five or six full meals a day inside of you for the next week. More if you can. The change consumes an enormous amount of fuel so make sure you keep the fires well stoked. Now, Nathan, show our young lady her room. She can meet everyone at dinner tonight after she's had time to have something to eat, then rest and bathe.'

Nathan nodded and led Emily back to her room, leaving her at the door. 'I'll send someone to fetch you for dinner,' he said. 'Seven o'clock. If you need a snack or actually, anything at all, there's a pull cord next to the bed. Give it a yank and a servant will come and tackle your order.'

The room was huge. More of a suite than a bedroom. A leather sofa, two wingback chairs, a coffee table, plus a four-seater dining table. A large flat-screen television and a dock for an iPod or iPhone. Emily had neither. She had never had any use for a cell phone and she had always streamed her music or played it on the old vinyl records Bart and Ryoko owned.

Her suitcase was placed on the end of her bed and when she opened it she found it to be empty. After checking the freestanding wardrobe on the one wall, she found all of her clothes already hung up or folded in the drawers.

She was surprised to find, apart from

the clothes she had brought with her, there were at least another five full outfits. All were a simple variation on a theme, black, thick cotton and leather, long coats, calf high boots. She tried one of the coats on. It was superbly tailored, snug fitting with no shiny buttons or any loose epaulettes or tags. Simple and elegant and practical.

It was obvious the outfits were some sort of a uniform. She opened the door that led to the bathroom. An oversized four-claw, freestanding tub graced the center of the room. In the corner a walk-in shower large enough for a troop of dancers, with a showerhead the size of a serving platter. Emily smiled happily and turned the water on. It cascaded from the head and thundered onto the tiles like a tropical monsoon as she stripped down and stepped into the steaming deluge.

The hot water was bliss as she soaped herself into a foaming lather, rinsed, turned the water off, and then donned a plush cotton robe that hung on the back of the door as well as slipping on a pair of white-flannel bath slippers.

As she went through to the bedroom she checked the time. Her watch said it was 5:48 but she quickly realized it was still on Alaskan time. That made it 1:48 local. Time for something to eat and then a nap before dinner.

She pulled the bell-cord but heard nothing and assumed the corresponding bell was too far away to register aurally. Surprisingly there was a knock on the door almost instantly, so she walked over and opened it. There stood a woman dressed in a classic Victorian maid's outfit. Long coarse black dress, lace up boots, a white pinafore over the top and a white frilly bonnet pulled down over her ears.

Emily smiled but the maid didn't react. She simply stood still and stared blankly ahead.

Eventually Emily spoke. 'Umm...hi. I'm rather hungry and I was hoping you may be able to fetch me something to eat.'

The maid turned away and walked off. Her movements steady and careful. Almost as though she was drunk and had to concentrate on keeping herself upright and mobile.

'Now that's an odd one,' said Emily to herself. 'Oh well, not long until dinner.'

There was a chill in the air after her shower, so Emily decided to light a fire and was happy to note it had already been laid. On a shelf next to the inglenook stood a wooden box of extra-long matches. She struck one and held it to the paper that stuck out from under the pile of logs and kindling. It took instantly, and, within a couple of minutes, the seasoned wood crackled and spat, filling the room with gentle, comforting warmth.

At the same time there was a knock on the door. She opened it to reveal the self-same maid, this time wheeling a trolley laden with silver cloche-covered dishes. Again, without talking, she wheeled the trolley next to the dining table and proceeded to lay out a full meal. The cloches were picked up to reveal a whole roasted chicken, steamed vegetables, fried potatoes, and a jug of thick gravy. Finally, a slab of chocolate cake and a small jug of cream.

Emily's mouth started watering as she thanked the maid. But once again there was no visible reaction, so she simply sat down and tucked in.

After she had eaten, Emily set the alarm on her wrist watch, staggered to her bed, dropped her robe, shucked off her slippers, and crawled under the goose-down duvet, falling asleep almost as her head touched the pillow. Jet lagged into peaceful oblivion.

Chapter 5

Nathan had fetched her for dinner. Unsure of what to wear, Emily had chosen one of the black outfits in her closet. Snug-fitting leather trousers that were as soft as velvet, a black tailored blouse and calf-length black boots. A midnight symphony in fashion.

As she cast her eyes over the people seated at the dining table, she was glad of her decision to dress in the clothes provided, as everyone else was also clad totally in black.

Ambros, who was seated at the head of the table, stood and greeted her as she entered.

'Emily, my dear, welcome.' He turned to address the others at the table. 'Good people, may I introduce Emily Hawk, our newest Shadowhunter.'

Aside from Nathan, there were five other people seated at the table. Four men and one woman.

Ambros started to introduce them.

'Lyle Potton,' he said. 'Another American.'

Lyle gave Emily a thumbs up. 'Yo, Emily.'

Emily nodded her acknowledgment of his greeting as she took quick stock of him. Lyle was huge. Not merely tall but also obscenely sumo-wrestler fat. His face a moon-like ball on top of a neck that consisted mainly of double chins above a barrel-shaped body. Arms and legs like tree trunks.

The next to be introduced was a wiry looking man, five ten, complete with dreadlocks and Rastafarian bead necklace, the red, yellow, and green standing out against the solemn black of his clothes.

His name was Bastian Miller and he stood and bowed deeply as he greeted Emily. 'My lady, it is an honor.'

Again, Emily nodded.

Next in line was the only other girl in the room. Josephine Brady. She was tiny with a build similar to Ryoko.

Her dark hair was long and lank, and

she wore makeup like it was a defensive mask, thick purple eye shadow, scarlet lips, and pale base. In her mouth an unlit cigarette.

She waved to Emily but didn't meet her gaze, her eyes flickering from side to side and head cocked. She reminded Emily of a bird. A falcon.

After Josephine had been introduced, the next man stood up. Karl Wagner. Both his guttural accent and his looks marked him as the quintessential German. Six-foot, pale blue eyes. Close-cropped blond hair. Very short back and sides. Round steel rimmed eyeglasses. Eyebrows so blond as to be almost invisible, giving him an expressionless look. Disconcerting and slightly disturbing.

The final Shadowhunter was a South African. Piet Van Staden. Six foot three and built like a pro-wrestler. His shoulders and biceps strained against the cotton of his shirt and his neck was so thick it made his head look fractionally too small. He sported a short-cropped beard and his eyes were black pebbles, his lips a cruel slash. On the left side of his face a vivid scar ran from temple to chin, like a purple lightning bolt. Emily could sense that, out of all of the people in the room, this was a very dangerous man. Easily the most dangerous human being she had ever met. His aura projected a barely constrained violence. As if he had literally been dragged straight from a battle in order to attend the dinner and he was less than happy about it.

When he spoke, it was as if he wasn't used to verbal communication, the words coming out in short, grammatically incorrect chunks.

'Hello, Emily. To meet you I is pleased. If anything you does need. Ask me. If I's can help, I will.'

'Thank you, Piet,' acknowledged Emily. 'That's very sweet of you; I'll bear that in mind.'

The big man grunted, blushed at the compliment, and then sat down heavily, scowling at the table in order to cover his embarrassment.

'Aah, Piet, you're so sweet. What an absolute angel, would you like a pat on the head,' teased Lyle as he made wet kissy sounds.

Piet glared at him and then shook his head disgustedly and went back to scowling at the table. Ambros ushered Emily to a chair between Nathan and Bastian and, as soon as she sat down, a procession of servants started to bring in the evening meal. And although she had eaten a mere couple of hours ago she was ravenous again.

Piles of inch thick rump steaks, fries, slices of smoked ham, corn on the cob, poached eggs, and Waldorf salad. Emily piled her plate high, noticing everybody else was doing the same. Except for Lyle who simply pulled one of the serving platters of steak over to his place setting, threw a diverse amount of sides on top of it and got to eating.

Emily watched him for a while, fascinated at how swiftly he was consuming his food. He worked like an automaton, both hands moving in concert, left, right, left. Shoveling food into his chewing jaws, swallowing, chewing, and swallowing again. An industrial garbage disposal unit.

He glanced up and noticed Emily watching him.

'This is how a real man eats,' he said, his mouth full of masticated steak. 'It's quite a turn on, isn't it?'

Before Emily could answer, Piet pointed at the huge man. 'Watch your mouth, fat boy,' he growled. 'Don't make me come over there and teach you some manners.'

Lyle sneered at the Afrikaner, but Emily noticed he didn't push the point.

The rest of the meal was spent in almost total silence and every time Emily attempted to strike up any sort of discussion it was met with a one- or two-word answer, followed by silence. After ten minutes she started to feel a little uncomfortable.

Eventually Nathan, sensing her discomfort, addressed her directly. 'Don't get disheartened,' he advised. 'It's always like this at meal times. The odd bit of sniping between Piet and Lyle…well, actually between someone and Lyle and then the rest is simply people stuffing their faces.'

'Jealousy,' interjected the fat man.

'People rib on me because they're consumed with envy. Six hundred pounds of concentrated Alpha male enters the room and the green-eyed monster rears its ugly head. No worries though,' he continued. 'When you're as attractive as me you just gotta learn to live with the cupidity. Fortunately, I'm a big enough man to take it.' He hoovered up a handful of fries as he spoke, displaying a mouthful of chewed potato.

Emily shuddered.

'Hey, you bong belly pickney slabba,' said Bastian, using the Jamaican vernacular. 'Shut your fat face or I come over there and stick my foot up your ass.'

'Talk English,' retaliated Lyle. 'I know you can.'

'Aah, kiss me backside you fassy hole.'

'Enough,' said Ambros. Both Bastian and Lyle immediately stopped their bantering and concentrated on their food again. Ambros shook his head and smiled at Emily. 'You'd think after a hundred years or so they would learn to stop acting like children, wouldn't you?'

Emily nodded.

'Anyway,' continued the old man. 'Nathan is correct, meal times are not great for socializing. Due to the massive calorific intake a Shadowhunter needs, they tend to view meals as simple refueling exercises.

Formal dinners are the exception. But never fear, you'll get to know everyone better tomorrow morning at training. I recommend you get a good night's sleep, I'm sure you are still more than a little jet-lagged. I'll send one of the chaps to show you to the dojo in the morning. Set your alarm for seven, ready by seven thirty.'

Emily nodded and then applied herself to her food like everyone else at the table as she scarfed down her meal like a trencherman.

Chapter
6

The dojo was vast. Big enough for at least sixty plus people to train comfortably. The seven Shadowhunters looked lost in the huge open space.

'Why is it so big?' Emily asked Bastian, who had shown her to the dojo after fetching her from her room.

'Times gone by there used to be many more Shadowhunters,' he answered.

'Where have they gone?'

Bastian shrugged. 'Depends on your belief system, I suppose. If you're a Buddhist, reborn. Christian, heaven. Muslim, resurrection. Me, I believe in Zion.'

'Hold on,' said Emily. 'You mean they're all dead?'

'As the Dodo,' confirmed Bastian.

'How?'

'It's one of those side effects you get when you spend your whole time fighting almost unkillable undead beings with fangs and claws. A lot of us end up underground in wooden boxes.'

'But aren't we supposed to be like superfast and megastrong?'

Bastian raised an eyebrow. 'You ever seen a vamp?'

Emily shook her head. 'I don't think so.'

'That would be a no then,' confirmed the Rasta. 'You would remember if you had. Well, we're fast and strong but they is faster. Maybe not stronger but close. Also, they heal real quick. I mean, so do we but they heal almost instantaneously. Makes them damn hard to kill.'

'So, what's the point then?' asked Emily. 'How can we beat them?'

Bastian grinned. 'We train. They may be quicker but we're meaner. We got skills, girl. And we got weapons. Silver edged swords, silver bullets, lots of firepower. Come on, train with me first, then you can spend a bit of time with Piet, he's number one with bladed weapons.'

Emily followed the Rasta to a sparring

mat on the side of the dojo, a standard twenty-six foot by twenty-six foot.

'Right,' said Bastian. 'Let's fight.'

Emily bowed and then assumed a standard Bow Stance or *Gong Bu*, leading leg in front and slightly bent, trailing foot angled at a forty-five-degree angle.

It was a great stance for attacking. The structure of it allowing her to punch with greater power by driving the rear leg into the ground as well as ensuring her rear leg could be quickly drawn forward for kicking attacks.

She waited for Bastian to assume a position before she started. But to her surprise he didn't. Instead he danced from side to side in front of her, his body position low, arms weaving a pattern in front of his chest as he moved. It was hypnotic. A snake charmer's flute to a cobra.

Then he rolled and jumped up, swinging his foot in a circle, and cracking it alongside Emily's head. She rocked sideways as the blow landed and then she swept her leading foot forwards in an attempt to unbalance him. But he was no longer there as he danced away, spinning, and rolling. A constantly moving target.

Again, he spun and struck, his foot connecting with Emily's knee, sending her crashing to the floor.

She rolled away and flicked her legs, springing back onto her feet as she did. Bastian danced sideways, tucking and rolling and jumping as he did.

Emily shook her head and then crouched low, assuming the stance of the Tiger, her hands clawed in front of her, muscles relaxed as she prepared for explosive power.

She knew she had to stop Bastian moving. Somehow, she had to get hold of him and then strike hard and fast as soon as she did.

Bastian noted her change of tactic and nodded his approval.

And then he blurred into movement, legs sweeping, fists striking, elbow and knees smashing into Emily as he spun around her at blinding speed.

She went down under a welter of blows and before she could pick herself up Bastian had her in a savage choke hold.

Just before she blacked out, Bastian let go, stood up and helped her to her feet. 'Breathe,' he said.

Emily took a deep breath and then socked the Rasta on the shoulder. 'What the hell? I thought we were sparring. What's with the whole kicking my butt thing?'

Bastian stared at her, his face deadly serious. 'Emily,' he said. 'At the Olympus Foundation when we train, we don't spar. We fight. Properly.'

'Why?'

'I assume you have sparred before,' countered Bastian.

'Every day,' admitted Emily.

'Not to put too fine a point on it,' continued Bastian. 'But it didn't do you much good, did it? I kicked your ass without even raising a sweat and I can see you're at least a first-degree black belt. Plus, the fact you're uber strong and fast.'

'Yeah, well, you wouldn't stand still. What's with all the dancing?'

'It's called Capoeira,' he answered. 'It's a fast and versatile martial art from Brazil. It was developed for fighting when you're outnumbered or at a technological disadvantage.' He somersaulted forward and flicked a kick over Emily's head to demonstrate. 'The style emphasizes using the lower body to kick, sweep and take down and the upper body to assist those movements as well as attacking. You use a series of complex positions and body postures which you chain together in an uninterrupted flow so you can strike, dodge, and move without breaking motion. Makes it seriously unpredictable. And when you're fighting a bunch of Vamps you gotta keep moving 'cause those suckers are as quick as crap out of a goose. Come on, I'll teach you.'

For the next four hours Bastian grilled Emily in the art of Capoeira, starting with the *Ginga*, a constant dancing motion that keeps the capoeirista in regular movement, making them a frustrating target for a forward-advancing opponent. Then he moved on to the various striking and defensive techniques, working her hard until her whole body was covered in ugly black bruises.

After four hours they all stopped for lunch, trooping off to the dining room where mountains of food awaited them. Breads, fruit, whole roasted chickens, rice, potatoes, and pulses.

Nathan sat next to Emily and ensured she had enough to eat and drink.

'Bastian working you hard, I see.'

Emily nodded. 'I look like I've been in a major automobile accident,' she quipped. 'I don't think there's a square inch of my body that hasn't got a bruise on it.'

'There might be,' interjected Lyle as he leered at Emily. 'Perhaps you should strip down, and I'll check for you.'

'Shut it, fat boy,' growled Piet.

'Up yours,' grunted Lyle as he shoved a whole potato in his mouth.

'Don't worry about the physical damage,' said Nathan. 'We all heal up real quick. By tomorrow morning there won't be a mark on you. In a few weeks' time, once you've fully changed, the bruises will heal almost instantly. Even deep cuts and bone breaks will mend in minutes.'

'Cool,' responded Emily. 'Will it still hurt like it does now?'

'Like buggery,' affirmed Nathan. 'We heal but we still feel pain just like anyone else. Mind you, the density of our muscle makes it much harder to hurt us. You'll find something that would slice into a normal person will barely deliver more than a shallow cut.'

When they had finished eating they headed back to the dojo.

All accept for Lyle who stayed seated as he crammed another chicken down, followed by almost a gallon of freshly squeezed orange juice. Piet slapped the fat man on the back of his head as he walked past him, but Lyle didn't even react, so entranced was he by his food.

Bastian walked next to Emily. 'For the rest of the day I want you to train with Piet,' he said. 'He's the best when it comes to weapons. Blades, staffs, throwing stars, that type of thing.'

'What about firearms?'

'No. Karl is the firearms expert. You can spend time with him tomorrow.'

'Okay. If you are the combat expert, Piet is the weapons guy and Karl is firearms – what is Josephine?' asked Emily.

'Tech geek,' answered Bastian. 'I mean, she can fight pretty good but she's beyond awesome when it comes to computers and such. You've gotta watch her though,' he continued. 'She's a sandwich or two short of a picnic basket. Very emotional, goes off for everything and anything. So, we try to keep her out of the field.'

'And dare I ask what Lyle excels at?'

'Strength. Bong belly boy is stronger than any two of us put together. Even Big Piet. I mean, Lyle is one of life's genuine assholes but he's good to have around in a fight. Like the hulk but without the green skin or the social graces.'

Emily grinned. 'Fair enough.'

When they got back to the dojo she paired up with Piet. He started her with a *Bo*. A six-foot-long, heavy Red Oak staff that was held with two hands and used as a spear, a sword, and a staff. Then they moved onto swords, especially the katana, a traditional Japanese Samurai weapon. After that they progressed to nunchuks, shuriken, throwing knives, and sling shots.

Emily had trained with all of the weapons before but the South African Shadowhunter brought a level of skill and expertise to their handling that transcended normality. It was as if every weapon was an extension of him. Another appendage as opposed to a separate weapon.

After four hours with him she was ready to drop from exhaustion. Piet finally stopped, collected the weapons up and nodded his approval. 'You're good,' he said. 'Well done.'

'I don't feel good,' returned Emily. 'I feel clumsy and uncoordinated. Like a beginner.'

Piet laughed. A gruff sound more like a dog's growl than an affirmation of amusement. 'Trust me,' he said. 'Right now, you are superior to any other human being in the world.'

'What about you?' questioned Emily. 'And the other Shadowhunters? And the vamps?'

'I said human beings,' answered Piet as he turned away. 'Now come on, let's go and eat.'

Chapter 7

The next ten days were pretty much the same.

They woke early, ate, went to the dojo and then, as far as Emily was concerned, people took turns beating her up.

Except for one morning when she was told to train with Lyle.

It surprised her. She was expecting a morning of sexual innuendo, crass comments, and self-importance. Instead, Lyle put her through a physical training routine that brought with it a new respect for the fat man. For all of his bravado he obviously worked hard at building his strength and Emily learned a lot about how to train to maximum efficiency, building both power and endurance.

At the end of the session she thanked Lyle and patted him on the back in a show of camaraderie.

'Oh ho,' he responded. 'Look who's trying to get close up and physical with the big man. Join the queue, girl,' he continued. 'But don't fear, there's enough of Lyle to go around no matter how many of you there are.'

Emily shook her head. 'You know, Lyle, you're a complete half-wit.'

The fat man blew a massive raspberry and left the dojo to look for a snack.

On the last of the ten days, Karl took her to the underground shooting range for her morning training.

The German laid out a selection of firearms on the table in front of the targets. Emily was familiar with most of the usual makes and calibers of handguns, but she had to admit that many of the weapons on the table were outside her area of prior knowledge.

Karl pointed as he explained. 'Desert Eagle, 50 cal auto pistol, Glock 10mm, Thunder Twelve shotgun revolver, Fostech semiauto shotgun.' He picked up a handful of mixed ammunition.

'Note all of the rounds are silver-tipped. Or, in the case of the shotguns, pure silver. You'll also see we don't bother with the smaller caliber weapons, 9mm, 38 specials and the like. If you're hunting for blood suckers, you need loads of muzzle velocity to take them down.

'My preference is the Desert Eagle. You might prefer the Glock. Slightly smaller handle. Easier fit. Also, a bit easier to conceal. The shotguns are a little bulky, even the Thunder Twelve, but we only use those if we're going on an overt mission. Full-scale attacks on a headquarters or such. Right,' he slapped a magazine into one of the Glocks and racked the slide. 'Let's boogie. Show me what you've got.'

Emily took the weapon and hefted it a couple of times to get the feel. She knew the Glock had an internal safety, so all she had to do was point and pull. She looked downrange at the man-shaped silhouette target, picked the pistol up and squeezed off a round. The slug went through the center of its head.

Quickly she burned off the rest of the rounds, banging off all fifteen in fewer than three seconds. Every shot struck the target in the head. It was exceptional shooting and she couldn't help but grin with satisfaction as she placed the empty pistol back on the table.

Karl nodded and picked up another two fully loaded Glocks, one in each hand. Then he faced the target and blazed away, pulling the triggers faster than seemed humanly possible. A veritable storm of silver-tipped lead tore through the target. As each weapon's slide racked back, he ejected the empty magazines, flipped the pistols into the air, grabbed two more full magazines from the table, rammed the magazines into the pistols as they came down and burned off another thirty rounds in less than two seconds.

The paper target had been totally shredded.

He turned to the flabbergasted Emily. 'As I said. Blood suckers take a lot of firepower to put down. But don't worry; we'll work on your technique.'

That afternoon Emily found herself in the library with Josephine Brady. The small, dark-haired girl was showing

Emily the computerized archives and setting her up with a password so she could access them whenever she needed. She also gave her an iPhone. She explained that she had tweaked the phone, adding an extra layer of security, boosting its reception, battery life, and storage capacity to around twenty times more than the factory model.

It also came with two hidden features the Apple Corporation would never have dreamed of. The flashlight setting had been amped up to include a powerful UV light, and if you pushed the on button and the bottom of the phone together, a compressed air cylinder shot a silver needle out to a range of twenty feet. Neither of these would be fatal to Vampires but Josephine explained they would definitely slow them down and give someone time to either escape or to get hold of a better weapon.

By the time the evening meal came around, Emily felt like her brain had exploded. Due to her new photographic memory she had remembered everything Josephine had told her but actually understanding it was a different kettle of fish. She simply hoped her mind would eventually sift through all of the info and make some sense of it over time.

But truth be told, it was with a heavy heart that Emily finally went to bed that evening. It seemed everyone was better at everything than she was. Her newfound strength, speed, and mind powers had seemed so awesome only a few days ago. Now she felt like the kid in the playground that always gets chosen last because no one wants the loser on their team.

If she had been a different sort of girl she may have cried herself to sleep. Instead she resolved to try harder.

Then she made sure the fire was built up and snuggled down for a good night's rest.

Chapter 8

Emily sat in Ambros' study across the desk from the old man.

His hair hung loose about his shoulders as opposed to his usual ponytail and he was thumbing a wad of tobacco into his pipe with a calloused and nicotine stained thumb. It had surprised Emily when she had seen all of the Shadowhunters smoked. But when she brought it up with Bastian he had simply laughed as he informed her the normal rules did not apply to them. They were immune to mortal disease, he explained. No cancer, no dementia. Not even the common cold. So, if they wanted to smoke it was merely a lifestyle choice. Not a health issue.

He had offered her a cigarette, but Emily simply couldn't get over her natural prejudice she held towards the cancer-sticks and she had refused. Bastian had chuckled and said he would give her fifty years or so and she would be an addict just like the rest of them.

Ambros finally got his pipe to take and he leaned back in his chair and worked up a head of smoke with a contented look on his face.

'So,' he said. 'How are you getting on?'

Emily shrugged. 'Okay, I suppose.'

'You suppose?'

The teenager nodded. 'I mean, I like it here. But, honestly, I feel a bit useless. Everybody is better at everything than I am. Bastian beats the crap out of me, Lyle's like more than twice as strong as me, Karl can shoot multiple weapons at once and Piet is like the Terminator. Not to mention Josephine, who's just the ultimate super-geek. I thoughtI was meant to be this super-hero, uber-mean dude but all I am is the playground nerd.'

Ambros raised an eyebrow. 'I see,' he said. 'Strange way to see things.'

'Maybe,' agreed Emily. 'But it's true.'

The old man shook his head. 'No, my dear girl,' he countered. 'It is patently not true. In fact, I would venture to say it is quite the opposite. Firstly, how long have you been training with the other Shadowhunters?'

'Ten days,' answered Emily.

Ambros nodded. 'Gosh. A whole ten days. How many days do you think Bastian has been training to perfect his art?'

'I don't know.'

'Well I do,' said Ambros. 'Approximately forty-six thousand days. When Karl started training with firearms, his first weapons were a Napoleonic era flintlock cavalry pistol and a Baker muzzle-loading service rifle. He has been shooting since before cartridges were invented. Before semiauto pistols and machine guns. That is a serious amount of practice.

And do you know Josephine actually knew Charles Babbage? The man who invented the first proto-computer back in the nineteen thirties. Piet fought against the British in the first and the second Boer wars back in the late eighteen hundreds. These people have put in serious time to perfect their skills, so you cannot be disheartened that they may be better than you.'

'What about Lyle?' interjected Emily.

Ambros grimaced. 'Lyle is…well, he's Lyle. He's actually a relative youngster. Thirty-five years old. But he's driven. Trains hard and, to be brutally honest, he's a bit of a freak.

Even without Shadowhunter powers he would be unbelievably strong. It's just one of those things. But I'll tell you something,' continued Ambros. 'After Lyle you are the strongest here. And another few facts that may interest you; you're pretty much second best at everything.

Bastian reckons you could take anyone here, except for him. Karl says you are the best shot he's come across for over a hundred years. And as for Piet, well let's just say he didn't say anything overtly bad about you, which is the closest you will ever get to a compliment from him.'

Emily didn't react.

The old man shook his head. 'Do you appreciate what I have just told you?' he asked.

Emily nodded. 'I think so. You're saying I'm not the best at anything. But that's what I've just been telling you.'

'No,' said Ambros. 'I'm telling you that you are almost the best at everything. Even though you are a mere stripling that has only had ten days training. I'm telling you that you are special. I'm telling you that you are the most amazingly talented Hunter I have come across since your mother and father. And I would venture you surpass even them. Emily,' he continued. 'You have the potential to be the very best of the best. The ultimate Shadowhunter.'

Emily smiled. 'Wow,' she said. 'Thanks. That's cool.'

'I'm sure it is,' affirmed Ambros.

'And what about Nathan?' asked Emily. 'Everyone seems to have a specialty except Nathan. What's his thing?'

Before Ambros answered Emily was sure she saw the tiniest flicker of sympathy cross his face. 'Nathan is a bit of an all-rounder,' he said. 'In the past he was referred to by all as "The

Fixer". He is gifted at arbitration, negotiation. A born diplomat. A politician, I suppose. He used to keep the gears greased between the Olympus Foundation and the government, the captains of industry, the news and entertainment moguls.'

'And now?' asked Emily.

'Now, things are different,' admitted Ambros. 'A hundred years ago, before the internet and social media, we didn't have to keep such a low profile. Obviously, we were a secret organization but there were many notables who were in the know, as it were. Basically, Nathan took care of these notables.'

'I see,' noted Emily. 'Wow, no wonder he hankers after the old days. Seems like a real come down. He was almost like the public face of the Foundation and now he's...well, an all-rounder.'

'Yes,' said Ambros. 'It has been a difficult transformation for Nathan. Anyway, now, that said, I think it's time for you to venture out into the field. Nothing too overt. A short trip to London. I'll send Bastian and Nathan with you. There are a few things I'd like you all to check up on. I'll explain fully before you leave. So, go to your room, pack a few outfits and be ready to leave after lunch.'

Chapter 9

Emily traveled to London with Bastian and Nathan, all three ensconced in the back of the Rolls, surrounded by leather and wood.

Nathan was his usual attentive self, ensuring Emily was comfortable and had something to eat and drink, but she could tell he seemed to be a little preoccupied with his own thoughts.

Bastian, on the other hand, became visibly more relaxed the further they got from the headquarters. When she mentioned this to him he laughed.

'I can't stand that old place,' he informed Emily. 'All those grotesque sculptures and musty old carpets and dark corners. Sucks, man. Wait until you see the London pad. It's the dogs.'

Emily raised an eyebrow. 'The dogs?'

'English expression,' explained Bastian. 'The dog's bollocks. Means it's seriously cool.'

'Whatever,' said Emily. 'Sounds gross. I didn't find the big house so bad. The servants were a bit weird though.'

Bastian actually shuddered. 'Man, I hate those dudes,' he said, quietly.

'Hate seems a bit extreme,' argued Emily. 'I mean, given, they're not the most communicative of souls.'

'That's because they don't have any,' said Bastian.

'What?' asked Emily.

'Souls,' continued the Jamaican. 'The servants don't have any souls.' He stared at the teenage girl. 'Man. You didn't know?'

'Know what?'

'The servant dudes at the manor. They're all zombies. Dead.'

Emily shook her head. 'Good one, Bastian,' she said. 'Not funny though.'

'He's not joking,' assured Nathan. 'Sorry, I should have told you. They've been around forever. Some of them for hundreds of years. That's why they don't talk or react. They can't, due to being …well…dead, I suppose.'

'No way,' insisted Emily. 'Zombies don't exist.'

'Sure,' interjected Bastian. 'Or vampires or werewolves or Shadowhunters.'

Emily lay back in her seat, her face pale with shock. 'But, aren't zombies all, like, rotting and gross and keen to eat your brains and stuff. I mean, what if they bite us?'

'You mean "Night of the Living Dead" type zombies? Like the movies?' clarified Bastian.

'Exactly,' agreed Emily.

'No way. That's not how it works. That Romero dude has a lot to answer for. Real zombies are made by the Obeah Man.'

'Okay,' acknowledged Emily. 'And who is the Obeah Man when he's at home?'

'I suppose you'd call him a witch doctor,' answered Bastian. 'Voodoo man. He reanimates dead folk, turns them into servants. The staff at the manor were turned many years ago by an Obeah Man that worked for the Vamps. Ambros rescued them and then just sort of took them on.'

'Wow,' exclaimed Emily. 'That's super

creepy.'

'It's worse than creepy,' said Bastian with feeling. 'It's slavery. They got no choice in the matter.' The Jamaican shook his head. 'Man, that slavery shit stopped almost two hundred years ago.'

Emily put her hand on Bastian's arm. 'They're dead, Bastian,' she said. 'Or undead, not sure. But they don't know they're slaves.'

'I know,' admitted the Jamaican. 'Still doesn't make it right.'

Emily sensed neither Nathan nor Bastian felt like speaking for a while, so she lay back in her seat and went over the meeting they had just had with Ambros before they left.

The Olympus Foundation did not work in a vacuum. They had many people on their payroll, notably many high-ranking policemen. Most of them had no real idea what the Foundation actually did but they all knew if something unusual came to light it would behoove them to contact Ambros and put him in the picture. And so it was that the old man had been forwarded a copy of some CCTV footage of a break in at an antique shop in London called the Kensington Antique Emporium.

The fact of the break in was not unusual in itself. What made the case stand out was, firstly, nothing was stolen. Even though the intruders had obviously searched for something, as was evident by the wholesale mess they left behind. And, secondly, it appeared they had somehow managed to sabotage a state-of-the-art surveillance system, rendering it useless as far as identifying anyone concerned. It was this sabotage that had mainly attracted the police chief superintendent's attention. While the footage seemed at first glance to be fine, whenever the actual perpetrators came into shot it appeared they were moving at ultra-high speed. Like a film that had been speeded up by a factor of ten.

Ambros had explained he wanted them to take a closer look at the incident. Interview the owner of the Emporium, case out the area and see if anything of interest came to light.

By the time Emily had gone over all of the new info that had been dumped on her, the Rolls had arrived at their destination.

A large block of Victorian Gothic apartments situated above St Pancras Station, London. The driver drove them into the underground parking garage and they took a private elevator up to the penthouse apartment.

They unpacked and while Bastian prepared a lunch, Nathan gave Emily a quick tour of the surrounds. The penthouse occupied the top two floors of the building. It featured five bedrooms, each with their own en suite and small sitting area. There was also a main dining room, a large lounge, a gourmet kitchen, and several spacious balconies that boasted sweeping views of the capital city.

Nathan also explained the apartment was fully serviced by the adjoining five-star Marriot Hotel and the Foundation had an open account, so food could be ordered from any of the multitude of restaurants if they wanted.

'So,' said Emily. 'No zombie servants

then.'

Nathan chuckled. 'Why do you think Bastian loves it here so much?'

The three of them ate in the kitchen. Cheese, bread, pates, cold cuts, and fruit.

'Right,' said Bastian after they had all had their fill. 'Let's get to Kensington and give this antiques place the once over. We can take the tube from here, easier than using the car.'

'I can't make it,' said Nathan. 'Got some personal stuff to attend to. But I'll be free tomorrow.'

Bastian shook his head. 'We're not here to do personal stuff, man. Business first then you can sort your crap out afterwards.'

'Calm down,' snapped Nathan. 'I've got stuff to do. Chill, it's not the end of the world. Anyway, you've got Emily and it's just a simple walk and talk. Not like you're going to need backup.'

Bastian shrugged. 'Fine. Go do your stuff. We'll see you later.'

Chapter 10

Bastian guided Emily through the intricacies of the London underground, buying her an Oyster card, ensuring she had enough money on it, and making sure she knew where to stand on the escalators.

Just before they had left the apartment, Bastian had handed Emily a leather wallet. Inside was a warrant card with her rank, name, and number. According to the card she was a DS, detective sergeant, in the Special Branch.

According to Bastian it was a genuine card, although if push came to shove and someone looked more deeply into it they would discover she wasn't actually a member.

But the Jamaican assured her it wouldn't get to that, so she need not worry. They merely carried the cards as it gave them a reason to question people without raising suspicion.

Under an hour later they were sitting in the Emporium's reception area, waiting for the owner.

And when he walked into the room he was nothing like Emily had expected. This was no insipid, eccentric, bespectacled purveyor of antiquities. Instead, the man who walked in towered over both her and Bastian. Around twenty-three years old, his brown hair short and clean but a little bit shaggy, like he had simply run his hands through it instead of using a comb. He wore a dark single-breasted suit that had obviously been handmade, as had his Oxfords. A pale-blue shirt offset his blue eyes, so pale as to resemble flecks of shattered ice. But even the well-cut lines of the suit could not disguise the cords of muscle that stood out in ridges on his arms and shoulders.

He walked towards them, confident and assured. His movements controlled. Economical. Graceful yet somehow unrefined. As if he was purposefully keeping himself in check.

'William Townsend,' he greeted,

shaking Bastian by the hand.

'Thank you for meeting with us, Sir William. I am DI, detective inspector, Bastian Miller and this is my associate, DS, detective sergeant, Emily Hawk.'

William grasped Emily's hand and she had to stop herself gasping. It was as though someone had run an electric current through her. And sudden images of his shirtless torso filled her mind. She blushed a high red and pulled her hand back like a scorched cat.

Sir William raised an inquisitive eyebrow. 'I'm sorry, Miss Hawk,' he said, his voice a low, husky growl. 'Are you alright?'

'Of course,' snapped Emily. 'Why wouldn't I be?'

William looked away, obviously slightly taken aback by her waspish reaction.

Emily felt an immediate urge to apologize. Grab him by the arm. Pull him towards her. But she quashed the feelings and tried desperately to assume a calm and professional demeanor.

God, Emily, she scolded herself. *Show*

some control. What the hell is wrong with you?

'Sir William,' interjected Bastian. 'I wonder, could we talk about the break in?'

'Of course. Not much to tell. I've given your lot at the station a copy of the CCTV. Seems to have been on the blink. Kept skipping forward or something. Pity. Although they didn't take anything. Most likely just a bunch of youngsters looking to trash a place. A few breakages, mirrors, vases, and such. All covered by insurance. Sorry, not much more I can say. Obviously, no one was here. Took place around midnight.'

'So, you're absolutely sure nothing was taken?' insisted Bastian.

William nodded.

'Well then, that's about it,' said the Jamaican. 'Oh, one last thing. Have you heard of any other similar robbery attempts in the area?'

'No. Sorry, nothing that I know of, although I certainly wouldn't take that as gospel. I don't actually spend a lot of time at the shop.'

'Thanks,' said Bastian as he turned to leave, beckoning to Emily as he did so.

Emily nodded her goodbye to William and followed Bastian from the Emporium.

As she got to the door, however, the tall man hurried after them.

'I'm sorry,' he said. 'But if I don't do this then I shall regret it for a very long time, of that I'm sure.'

Bastian looked at him quizzically, wondering what information he was going to give up now. 'Go ahead, Sir William. What would you like to tell us?'

'Well, nothing. I mean, nothing to tell.' He looked a little abashed. 'What I mean is…' he hesitated and bit his bottom lip. 'Miss Hawk,' he continued. 'I was just wondering if…perhaps you might…on the off chance…possibly be free tomorrow night. You know. To go out. Dinner. With me. And you of course. I mean…the both of us.'

Emily blushed again and then cursed herself internally for doing so.

'Of course, Sir William,' she said. 'That would be great.'

The tall man looked disappointed. 'Oh, well. Yes. Of course. Sorry, I just thought it was worth an ask. You know. Nothing ventured and all that. Silly of me really.'

Emily laughed. 'I said yes.'

William's grin was a pleasure to behold as it spread over his face, lighting up his eyes and revealing his strong, white teeth. 'Of course you did. Splendid. Right, I'll pick you up tomorrow at eight.'

'Fine,' agreed Emily.

'Where?' asked William.

Emily gave him the address to the apartment in St Pancras and then she and Bastian took their leave.

As they walked away from the Emporium, towards the tube station Bastian chuckled under his breath. 'You know, Emily,' he said. 'You can control that.'

'What?' asked Emily, suddenly paranoid that Bastian had somehow perceived her visions of William's naked torso or noticed her electric reaction to the tall man's touch.

'Blushing,' he continued. 'It's simply a

visible manifestation of the physiological rebound of the basic instinctual fight or flight mechanism when physical action is not possible.'

'I wasn't blushing,' she denied.

'Course you were,' affirmed Bastian.

'Well what if I was,' continued Emily. 'You're saying it's a flight or fight response. Not true, I didn't want to fight William and I certainly didn't feel an urge to run away.'

'That was just a simplification,' said Bastian. 'What I meant was that it was triggered by an emotional stimulus. Fear, embarrassment, anxiety. Whatever, you figure out what emotion is causing it, once you know that then you can control it. Easily. After all, we are Shadowhunters. We're meant to be able to control our emotions and stuff. So, work on it.'

'Up yours,' grinned Emily. 'I've got better things to worry about.'

'True,' laughed Bastian. 'Tell you what, let's split up. We need to visit as many antique places as we can. See if there have been any similar occurrences compared to the break in at the Emporium. I really want to know what that bunch of blood suckers were searching for. Obviously, they didn't find it at Sir William's place, so odds are they'll keep looking. Unless our posh friend was lying, but I don't think he was. Anyway, you can take the opportunity on your date to grill him a bit more. See what you can get out of him.'

'We'll see,' said Emily. 'Okay, I'll head this way and you go that way.

I reckon we pop into any place that looks as if it sells old or interesting stuff. Check if they've had any break ins and question them as to what they've heard or what they might know about Sir William's break in.'

'Suits me,' agreed the Jamaican. 'Look, if you keep heading in that direction, eventually you'll come to central London. Soho, Leicester Square, so on. It's also going to get dark soon, around four o'clock. When you're done, get a cab back to the apartment and we can consolidate our info there. Right?'

Emily gave a thumb up. 'Right.'

Chapter 11

After a couple of hours, it became obvious to Emily she wasn't going to luck out with any relevant information. All she could glean from the people she interviewed was that Sir William was known to all but not actually known by anyone. He was highly respected and considered to be the best at what he did.

She kept walking towards central London but, soon after speaking to the tenth shop owner, she gave up on her information gathering and assumed the role of a young tourist in London for her first time. She marveled at the ancient buildings, the narrow alleyways, the black cabs, and the red double-decker buses.

Pubs with names like "The Slug and Lettuce" or "the Walrus and the Carpenter" or Emily's favorite – "The

Dirty Dick".

Bobbies on the beat with their tall custodian helmets. World renowned department stores like Harrods and Liberty and Hamley's. She also stopped outside almost every designer clothing store and lusted after the dresses and accessories inside. Clothes designed purely for beauty, with not an iota of care paid to their practicality. Proper girl clothes.

And before she knew it, the sun had set, and she was lost. A light drizzle filled the air with moisture, refracting the neon lights into a million tiny rainbows and beading on her hair and clothes in little crystal spheres. The streets around her were a lot less salubrious than the ones she had been walking along earlier and there were a lot less people around.

She walked to the end of the alley to discover it was a dead end, so she took out her phone and brought up her SatNav. It showed she was in the center of an area called SOHO. The London Town guide called it "The Sleazy Heart of London's Theater land". But she wasn't exactly nervous. After all, she justified to herself, this wasn't downtown Laos or Sarajevo. It was the center of one of the capital cities of the first world.

But every city has an underbelly. And therein live the bottom feeders. Petty thieves, bums, hookers, and con artists. Or simply forgotten men looking for trouble, keen to stamp their faded authority on whoever they could, in an effort to bolster their own low self-esteem.

In essence – assholes.

And now there were five of them blocking the exit to the narrow alley.

'Lost are we, girly?' asked one of the men, his round face shiny with rain and his shaved head aglow from the neon lights.

'No thanks,' answered Emily. 'I'm fine.'

'Oh, American, are we?' asked the man. 'Good. I like American girls.'

There was a chorus of appreciative laughter amongst the other men. A pack of hyenas. Followers.

They walked closer, spreading out as they came in order to block all possibility of escape.

Emily's enhanced senses could pick up their smell. A rank combination of stale beer and unwashed body odor. Her heart rate sped up, thumping frantically in her chest. Then she remembered she was no ordinary girl. Not anymore. And if anyone in the alley should be nervous it certainly wasn't her.

She felt her anger well up inside her and she started to walk towards the approaching thugs.

'Steady, girly,' quipped the leader. 'Bit keen, aren't we?'

More moronic laughter echoed around the alley.

Emily took a few more steps until she was a mere two feet from the chief scumbag. 'So, you wanna play?' she asked. The man looked a bit puzzled. And for the first time his arrogance slipped a little as Emily's supreme level of confidence washed over him.

Emily winked at him. 'Might as well,' she said. 'I mean, I'm in London to do the sights and kick some ass. And I've already done the sights for today.'

Her right hand whipped out in an open

hand palm strike to the man's temple. His eyes rolled back in his head and he slumped to the ground. A puppet with its strings cut.

The laughter amongst his men died down as their limited cerebral capacity attempted to catch up with the rapidly changing flow of events.

Emily stood still and let her eyes run over the motley crew. 'Well then, boys,' she said. 'Who's next?'

Two men attacked at once. But to Emily it was as though they were moving in slow motion. Their movements sluggish and clumsy. Toddlers playing at being adults.

She didn't even bother to get technical with them and simply slapped them both on the side of their heads with her open hands.

Left. Right. Both of them flew backwards, hit the ground, and lay still.

Whether they were unconscious or not did not enter into the equation. They had obviously both decided that, for them, the fight was most definitely over.

Then the next man made a mistake. His

hand dipped into his jacket pocket and came out holding a stiletto. The six-inch blade flashed silver in the overhead lights as he waved it from side to side in an effort to intimidate.

Emily shook her head. 'Put it away. Trust me,' she urged. 'You don't want to go there. Put it down and walk away. Fun's over.'

He jumped forward, leading with the blade, striving to cut. To wound.

Emily moved to the side, letting his knife arm slip past and then she swiveled, flicked her leg up and brought it crashing down on the man's right shoulder. She heard the collar bone splinter as her kick landed and she readied herself for another strike. But it wasn't necessary as he collapsed in a heap, the knife slipping from his nerveless fingers and skittering away into the gutter.

The final assailant put both his hands up, turned and ran. Leaving his wounded and broken companions to fare for themselves.

Emily spent a minute putting all of the unconscious men into the recovery position, ensuring they were breathing freely and there was no possibility of their airways becoming obstructed.

Then she left the alley and hailed a cab to take her back to the apartment.

Chapter 12

'**O**ver six hundred years of combined wisdom between the five of you and this is the result,' said Radford Cromwell, the head of the *Nosferatu* Enforcers.

'With all due respect, master,' answered one of the Aspirants who knelt in front of the Enforcer. 'We were told Sir William might have had the relic. We were simply searching for it.'

The Enforcer glided across the floor and stood in front of the kneeling Aspirant. He looked down at him, an expression of utter disgust on his face as his fangs extended, sliding past his lower lips.

'With all due respect,' he whispered. He bent down, his face now level with the terrified junior vampire.

'You have no concept of what respect is, you worthless leech. Did I tell you to search the Emporium?'

The Aspirant shook his head.

'Did Lord Byron instruct you to do it?'

'No, sir.'

'Correct. So why did you and your gaggle of moronic parasites break into a place covered by closed circuit television and then not even bother to remove the evidence?'

'There was no way the cameras could have identified us, my lord Enforcer,' answered the Aspirant. 'We moved far too fast.'

The Enforcer stood up. 'Oh well. That's fine then. Not a problem. Too fast for the cameras you say?'

'Yes, sir.'

'Faster than a human is capable of moving?'

'Much faster, my lord,' agreed the Aspirant.

The Enforcers hand flashed forward, claws extended. The razor-sharp talons tore through the kneeling Aspirant's neck, separating his head from his shoulders in one single mighty blow. The severed cranium bounced along the floor until it rolled to a stop against the wall with a dull thud.

Cromwell grabbed the next Aspirant by the neck and picked him up one handed. 'And now, because of you swarm of cretins, somebody out there has photographic proof of someone, or something, that can move ten times faster than a human being.'

'My Lord,' rasped the Aspirant who was still suspended by his neck. 'I am sure they will merely think the cameras have malfunctioned. No one will believe what they see.'

'No one?' bellowed Cromwell. 'No, not "No One". Most humans will not believe. But there are some that will. In fact, there are some that will know exactly what they are seeing. And those are the very people we do not want looking into what we are doing.'

'With a casual shrug of his shoulders the Enforcer separated the Aspirant's head from his shoulders. Tearing it off like he was plucking an over ripe fruit from a tree. He tossed both head and body aside before turning to the remaining two kneeling Aspirants.

'Get out before I destroy you,' he growled.

The two juniors sprang to their feet and ran from the room, their bodies a blur from the speed at which they moved.

Cromwell stood still for a while as he pondered. He wasn't worried about Sir William as such. The man was a mere human. Weak. Nothing more than prey. No, he was more concerned about who else might see the CCTV footage. Namely – the Olympus Foundation.

It was true they were no longer the force they used to be a full century ago. Their numbers had dropped as the vastly superior numbers of the brethren had slowly whittled away at them.

Oh, the house of Lord Byron had lost many hundreds, if not thousands, of brethren to the blades and bullets of the Shadowhunters.

But unlike them, vampires could beget more vampires. Whereas the Olympus Foundation was stuck with a slowly dwindling line of succession that was literally dying out.

But they could still cause untold problems, thought Cromwell to himself. Especially that disgusting old magician. He had been a thorn in the brethren's side for centuries now. An unacceptable situation as far as the Enforcer was concerned. In fact, he continued to think, it was time to approach the Grand Master with the plan that Cromwell had been working on. A plan to eradicate these so called Shadowhunters and their despicable leader, once and for all.

A purge, as it were.

Cromwell smiled to himself. And his canines shone as white as innocence in the darkling light.

Chapter 13

When she had arrived back at the apartment the night before, Emily had decided not to tell Bastian or Nathan about her run in with the thugs in Soho. No harm had been done to her and she was afraid the men would overreact and put some sort of curfew on her.

'I got no girl clothes,' she said to no one in particular, as she entered the sitting room the next morning.

'What do you mean?' asked Nathan. 'You have clothes. That's what you wear every day.'

Emily rolled her eyes. 'I'm meant to be going on a date tonight and all I have is jeans and T-shirts or our black Shadowhunter outfits. I mean, they're pretty cool but I don't want to go out to some fancy place looking like I've just walked off the set of The Matrix.'

'Going out on a date?' asked Nathan. The surprise sounding clearly in his voice.

'Yeah,' confirmed Emily. 'What? You think I'm too hideous to be invited out?'

'No.' Nathan shook his head. 'It's just, well, who is he? Or she, whatever. You've only been in London for a day. How did this happen. Is it safe?'

'It's all cool,' interjected Bastian. 'Some posh nob who owns the Antique Emporium we went to yesterday. You would know if you actually did any work instead of swanning about on your own private business instead.'

'I wasn't swanning about,' denied Nathan. 'I had stuff to do.'

'Sure,' countered Bastian as he stood up. 'Tell you what,' he said to Emily. 'Let's go out. You got a Foundation debit card; we'll use it to buy you some "Girl Clothes".'

'The card is not for frivolities,' snapped Nathan.

'Lighten up, dude. Stop being such a fassy-man. The girl needs some clothes and the Foundation got more money than god, so shut your pie hole, right?'

Nathan held his hands up. 'Fine then,

whatever. But let it be known I don't approve.' He stood up and went through to his room, slamming the door behind him.

'Wow,' exclaimed Emily. 'Who put a bug up his ass?'

Bastian grinned. 'I think our Canadian boy is jealous.'

'Of what?' asked Emily.

'Don't be so dense,' answered Bastian.

Emily blushed. 'Oh,' she said. 'But, we're just friends. I mean, I hardly even know him.'

'So? You don't know William either and you're going on a date with him.'

'That's different.'

Bastian shook his head. 'No. Not really. And you still haven't worked out how to control that blush response of yours.'

Emily stuck her tongue out.

'Charming,' laughed the Jamaican. 'Let's go. We got some plastic to bend.'

Emily spent the rest of the day choosing clothes and accessories, helped by the surprisingly knowledgeable Jamaican. When she commented, he informed her that he had grown up as one of seven children. And he had been the only male.

When Emily had enquired where the rest of his family was now he had simply shaken his head. She could see by the look of anguish in his eyes that bad things had happened. She grasped his shoulder in mute understanding and he smiled back at her in appreciation of her sympathy.

That afternoon Emily arrived back at the apartment with three separate outfits complete with matching accessories and, after much deliberation, she decided on the one she was going to wear that evening.

At half past seven she emerged from her bedroom, fully dressed and ready for the first date she had ever had. Nerves chewed at her stomach and caused her heart to flutter madly in her chest and, for a moment, she actually contemplated calling the whole thing off.

She walked into the sitting room and stood still, waiting for some sort of comment from either Bastian or

Nathan. Hoping it would be complimentary.

Or at least not insulting.

Bastian stood up as she entered the room and he gave a long, low whistle. 'Hey, all de fruits are right, girl,' he said. 'Looking fine with a capital F.'

She wore a figure-hugging, knee-length white and red Ted Baker cocktail dress with a pair of red Christian Louboutin stilettos and a simple silver necklace with a red garnet teardrop crystal pendant. The ensemble was finished off with a small red Vivienne Westwood clutch bag in a textured glitter finish.

Emily giggled 'Thank you, Bastian.'

Nathan stood up. 'You look…' he hesitated. 'Stunning.'

Emily turned to thank Nathan but before she could he had already left the room and headed to his bedroom, once again slamming the door behind him.

Bastian shrugged and shook his head. 'Just ignore him,' he advised Emily.

Before Emily could answer there was a buzz from the lobby intercom. She went over to the screen and took a look. Standing next to the concierge was an old man with a chauffeur's cap on. The concierge spoke into the intercom. 'Ma'am, your ride is here.'

'I'll be down now,' confirmed Emily. 'Man,' she said as she left. 'What is it with this country, does everybody have a chauffeur?'

Bastian laughed. 'Hardly,' he answered. 'Have fun. Don't do anything that I would.'

'As if,' countered Emily as she stepped into the private elevator.

She and the chauffeur went down and then she followed the ancient driver out of the building to the waiting car. William stood outside and waved to her as she approached.

He kissed her briefly on each cheek in the French fashion and then opened the door, holding her elbow as she slid onto the back seat. Then he walked around the back of the car and climbed in next to her. Meanwhile the chauffeur had gotten behind the wheel and they pulled out into the traffic.

The car was a Bentley Continental R, a massive beast of an automobile, almost eighteen feet long and twelve feet wide.

The interior was as plush as a gentleman's club and so silent that the only sound was the tick of the carriage clock that was sunk into the walnut paneling above the small bar.

William pushed a button and the strains of Miles Davis filled the cab, the sultry tones offsetting the nervous flutter his brief kisses had set off in Emily's chest.

'Nice,' she said. 'Miles Davis, Porgy and Bess. Released March the 9th, 1959. This was one of his first modal compositions. Instead of soloing in the straight, conventional, melodic way, his new style of improvisation featured rapid mode and scale changes played against sparse chord changes. A real break from the norm.'

William raised an eyebrow. 'So, I take it you are a huge jazz fan.'

'No, not really,' admitted Emily. 'It's just that I know stuff. Well, I remember stuff. All sorts of stuff. Everything, actually.'

Emily realized she was babbling, but for the life of her she couldn't stop. It was like the words were tumbling out of her mouth in an attempt to sabotage her date by convincing the tall, good looking man next to her, that she was a complete airhead.

'Sorry,' she apologized. 'I'm prattling on. Must be nervous or something.'

William laughed. 'Do you get nervous on all of your dates?'

Emily shrugged. 'No. I mean, maybe. Not sure. Actually, I've never been on a date before.'

Inwardly she cursed herself. *Great*, she thought. *Now he knows you're a complete nerd and you've lived the life of a recluse. Darn it.*

'Well there's no reason to be nervous,' assured William. 'We're just two people going to get a bite to eat. You look really nice, by the way,' he continued. 'Smashing. So how come you've never gone on a date before?'

'It's a long story. Short version is, I lost my parents when I was quite young, so I had to move in with two family friends. They were great, but they lived in the middle of nowhere. No people, therefore, no dates.'

'I see, sorry about your parents. I too have lost mine.'

'Sucks, doesn't it. I mean, Bart and Ryoko are great. Really lovely, but they're not my mom and dad. I miss my parents. Do you still miss yours?'

William shrugged. 'I lost them so very long ago. Decades.'

'Couldn't have been that long,' pointed out Emily. 'Hell, you can't be more than twenty-three, twenty-four.'

William scowled. 'Of course. I mean, it seems like decades. Years and years.'

'Yeah,' agreed Emily. 'Sometimes it does.'

The driver pulled over in front of a large, solid-looking building on the banks of the river Thames. On the top of the edifice Emily could make out a sign that read OXO.

The chauffeur opened the door for her and she followed William into the building.

When the exited the elevator on the top floor they were greeted by a young man in chefs' whites.

He bowed to William and then led them through the restaurant and into the kitchen. Then he showed them to a small table situated next to a plate glass window that overlooked the river, the lights of London diffused into smears of color from the light rain.

Another man came bustling up. He was also dressed in chefs' whites and he greeted William with a hug. William introduced him as Jeremy and the chef kissed the back of Emily's hand.

'Sit, sit, sit,' he urged. 'I bring food and wine. You relax.'

Within minutes a bottle of wine arrived and was presented to William. He glanced at the bottle and nodded his approval.

The sommelier opened it, tasted it using a *tastevin* that hung around his neck, poured a glass for each of them and left. Soon after, food began to arrive.

It was obvious Jeremy was sending them whatever he thought worthy of their special attention. Scallops in a white wine reduction on a bed of Pok Choi, Slices of lobster in a truffle sauce, rare Kobe beef fillet with brandy cream, asparagus, and wild mushroom risotto. Multiple small portions of exquisite culinary genius.

As the evening wore on, Emily found herself more and more at ease. William was the consummate host, charming and attentive as well as being a great raconteur.

It was only when the dessert of handmade chocolates arrived that Emily realized she still knew very little about the handsome man sitting opposite her. Every question she had asked had either been only superficially answered or gently deflected. He had told many entertaining stories but none of them were about himself.

Over coffee and liqueurs, she made a last concerted effort to pry some personal information out of William. But, once again, he replied in non sequiturs, or simply reversed the question so she ended up talking about herself again.

In the end she gave up trying and, instead, simply reveled in his company as she enjoyed herself more than she had since she could ever remember.

Later that evening, when he dropped her back at the apartment, he had kissed her goodnight.

And when she climbed into bed she could still feel the touch of his lips against hers. Soft yet firm at the same time. As hot as fever and as cold as ice. She smiled to herself as she slipped into slumber.

Chapter 14

When Emily woke the next morning, she found she was alone in the apartment. Both Nathan and Bastian had gone out without leaving her a message. At a bit of a loose end, she spent the day training and then walking around the local area, doing her tourist thing once again.

As the sun was dropping below the skyline she headed back, looking forward to a coffee and something to eat.

When she got into the kitchen Nathan was already there, sitting at the table, hands clasped around a mug of steaming tea.

He glanced up at Emily as she walked in.

And for the briefest moment she was sure she saw a look of pure hatred flash in his eyes.

But then he stood up and greeted her

warmly, enquiring as to how her date had gone and she figured she must have imagined it.

'Went great,' she smiled. 'William was a real gentleman. Good food, good company. Nothing wrong.'

'I'm glad,' returned Nathan. 'Look, I've come across a bit of info regarding the vamp break-in at the Emporium. I need to go and meet with an informant of mine, down at the docks near the Isle of Dogs. I don't know where Bastian has got to and I'd really appreciate some backup. Do you think you could come along?'

Emily nodded. 'Sure, Happy to.'

'Excellent. Get a coffee, get something to eat, and then we'll tool up and be on our way.'

Emily bolted down a huge bowl of fruit and nut muesli and a mug of coffee while Nathan went to the arms safe and took out a pile of weapons. He laid them on the table and pushed a selection across to Emily.

A Katana Japanese sword, two throwing knives, one strapped to each arm, and a heavy dagger to go on her belt. The Katana slipped into a specially designed shoulder rig so it hung under her left arm, concealed by her leather jacket.

As usual, all of the bladed weapons were impregnated with silver.

'We won't take any firearms,' said Nathan. 'I don't really expect anything to go down and, anyway; we wouldn't want to start a firefight in the city.'

The two Shadowhunters took the elevator to the underground car park and Nathan showed Emily to a black Range Rover, pressing the key fob to unlock the doors as they walked towards it.

It took almost an hour to crawl through the city traffic and down to the Isle of Dogs. Nathan found a parking space in a tatty side street and then Emily followed him through a veritable maze of alleyways.

Above them loomed the massive glass and concrete edifices of the office blocks at Canary Wharf, diametrically contrasting with the narrow shabby streets around them. Nathan led the way to a row of Victorian terrace houses. They stood under a flickering street lamp and waited for Nathan's snitch to arrive, turning their collars up against the seemingly ever-present drizzle that permeated the London air.

Nathan kept shifting from foot to foot, eyes constantly searching the area around them. Ill at ease and nervous. Emily wondered why he was acting so anxious but put it down to the fact he must be worrying about his informant showing up.

After almost half an hour Nathan shook his head.

'He should have arrived by now,' he said.

'Look, can you stay here in case he pitches up? I'm going to have a scout around, see if I can find him. Okay?'

Emily nodded and leaned against the lamp post in an effort to make herself less uncomfortable as Nathan jogged off around the corner.

Without warning, the lamp above her shattered and the street went dark. Emily jumped but then figured it was simply an old bulb giving up the ghost. Nevertheless, her senses ratcheted up a few notches as her heart rate increased. Colors stood out as more vibrant, the sound of the people living in the wretched, dilapidated houses came across clearly, like they were talking next to her.

Then a strange smell accosted her nasal passages. An overlying hint of snow with an undercurrent of something rotten. Dead.

Out of the corner of her eye she sensed movement. A mere flicker. A shadow. She turned to look but it was gone. And then, appearing in front of her as if by magic, stood four figures. Dressed like her, all in black. Three men and a woman. Their faces as white as a shroud. Lips blood red and eyes like dead coals.

The one man smiled, and Emily could plainly see his two large fangs sticking out an inch over his bottom lip.

She felt as though someone had just thrown a bucket of ice cold water over her. Her mind shrieked, telling her to run.

But her legs simply couldn't move. She was literally glued to the spot by an overwhelming feeling of terror.

Vampires.

She tried to call out to Nathan, but her voice merely vanished in her throat.

The lead vampire shook his head. 'Goodness me,' he said. 'Has the mighty Olympus Foundation come to this? Taking on terrified little girls to become Shadowhunters.' He laughed, and the other blood suckers joined in. Their lyrical laughter, proof they were genuinely amused at how low the Foundation had sunk.

At how pathetic they thought the new Shadowhunter was.

'So, this is what they think will stop us searching for the *corona potestatem?*' sneered the female vampire. 'I'm almost embarrassed for them.'

A wave of rage washed over Emily as she noted the scorn in the vampire's expressions.

'That's it, you Dracula wannabees,' she growled. 'I don't care who or what you are, I'm gonna be taking names and chopping heads off.'

She drew her Katana as she spoke and the silver-coated blade shone in the wan moonlight, shimmering like it was magically charged.

The lead vampire hissed as he sensed the silver but still he moved forward. Emily kept the sword in front of her, tracking the vampire as he approached.

Then the other three blood suckers split up, one flanking to Emily's right and the other two to her left. She knew they were all going to pounce at once and overwhelm her, so she decided to take the fight to them instead and leapt forward, swinging her Katana in an overhead strike as she did so.

But the lead vamp moved out of the way with such breathtaking speed that Emily lost sight of him.

Remembering Bastian's advice, Emily kept moving, somersaulting forward and then rolling to her right as she hit the ground. She swung her blade again as she did so and felt a satisfying shock as the silver-steel cut into something. As she jumped to her feet again she saw the female vampire stagger away from her, gouts of blood jetting from her right arm.

She moved again, desperately scanning

about as she tried to pick up where the other three vamps were, but she wasn't quick enough, and something seemed to explode against the side of her head.

She went down hard, rolling as she did but her vision blurred in and out of focus and she could feel blood trickling down from her temple and onto her cheek. She realized one of the vamps must have punched or kicked her.

Emily whipped her Katana around her head, more in a desperate attempt to keep her attackers away than anything else.

The three unharmed vamps appeared in front of her once again and, out of the corner of her eye she noticed the female was still bleeding but it appeared as if her cut was starting to heal.

Feelings of panic started to flutter on the edges of Emily's consciousness as she wondered what the hell she was going to do next. She was outnumbered and, as far as she could tell, outclassed by the bevy of blood suckers.

She moved again, pushing herself harder than she ever had before, dropping to the ground, rolling forward, and coming up hard and fast, punching upwards with the katana as she did. The blade struck the lead vampire in the center of his stomach and penetrated all the way through his body, emerging from his back in a spray of deep red blood. But as he fell forward the sword was ripped out of Emily's grasp and she had to retreat, drawing her heavy dagger as she did so. The skewered blood sucker glared at her as she skipped away from him. Then, with a grimace of pain on his face, he slowly pulled the sword from his torso and cast it aside.

'Now you've gone and pissed me off,' he spat. His voice a sibilant hiss of pure white-hot anger. He coughed, and blood splattered onto the pavement. Then he shook himself like a dog, threw his head back and howled. A high-pitched keening sound that set Emily's teeth on edge and brought on an instant head ache.

A wave of pure terror washed over the young Shadowhunter as she realized that this was it. But then she immediately quashed the feeling, sucked in a lungful of air, and braced herself. If she was going to die, then she was going to do her damndest to take out at least one of these disgusting human leeches before she did.

As one, the vampires attacked. Moving at blistering speed, with fangs and claws extended, ready to slash and tear and bite.

But just before they struck there was a flash of silver and the lead vampire's head leapt from his shoulders in a huge fountain of blood. A blur of shadow and the other three blood suckers were thrown back as something smashed into them. Emily breathed a sigh of relief, thinking Nathan had come to her rescue but as she looked up she instantly saw it was not her friend.

Instead, she saw another vampire, his fangs glistening in the moonlight, talons extended. In his right hand a slim razor-sharp rapier that dripped blood.

The remaining three vampires snarled and hissed as they prowled back and forth, eyeing the newcomer with trepidation.

Then he struck again, his movement a smear of darkness in the night. Talons tore open the female vampire's throat and the rapier finished off the job, slicing her head cleanly off.

The last two vamps turned to run but the newcomer leapt high into the air and came down on them, slashing downwards with his sword as he did, skewering the one blood sucker through his neck and deep into his torso. Then with a sickening crunch the newcomer jerked the blade from side to side, tearing open a massive wound that dropped the vamp to the ground. As he fell the newcomer grabbed his head and twisted it violently, ripping it off as he did so. Within seconds he had dispatched the final blood sucker in a similar fashion.

Then he stood and faced Emily.

The wind made his black cloak billow about him and the moonlight reflected off his deep green eyes. His long black hair hung down past his shoulders and his pale face was unshaven. His lips, full and sensual and as red as blood. His skin as pale as an angel of the grave.

He was quite possibly the sexiest man Emily had ever seen in her life.

And then his eyes flashed, and, with a whisper of air, he was gone.

Emily turned as she heard running footsteps. It was Nathan, sprinting down the road towards her. 'My god,' he shouted as he drew close and saw the carnage around his fellow Shadowhunter. 'What the hell? Are you alright?' He grabbed Emily by the shoulders, running his hands over her as he checked for any wounds.

'I'm fine' she answered in a shaky voice.

'Come on, let's get out of here,' responded Nathan as he dragged Emily back to their car. He opened the door for her and then he got into the driver's seat. Before he pulled off he took out his cell phone and made a call.

'Ambros, it's Nathan. We've had an incident. Belgrade Street, Isle of Dogs. Need cleanup as soon as. Four bodies, vamps. They've been decapitated.' He paused for a few seconds and the spoke again. 'No, it was Emily,' he said. 'I'll get her back to the apartment. Speak to you later.'

Then, without further ado, Nathan, ended the call, started the car, and set off back to St. Pancras.

Chapter 15

Bastian slammed his fist down on the table, cracking the two-inch-thick oak as if it were fine china. 'What were you thinking?' he shouted at Nathan. 'She's a bloody child and you put her in harm's way. Why did you leave her there?'

'She survived,' countered Nathan with a sulky look on his face. 'Not sure how, but no harm no foul.'

'Jesus, Nathan. Don't be so blasé about this. You took an amateur into a battle zone.'

'I didn't know it was a battle zone. I thought she'd be fine.'

'Hey guys,' interrupted Emily. 'I am right here you know. Don't I get a say in this. Also, Bastian, I'm not a child.'

The Jamaican shook his head. 'You're eighteen years old. Nathan and I are both over one hundred years older. You *are* a child.'

Emily stuck her tongue out at him. 'Look, Bastian, I'm fine. Thanks for the concern but it worked out okay. So, let's drop it.'

Bastian pointed at Nathan. 'I'm not happy, Nathan,' he said. 'This isn't over. You and I need to go round and round for a while.'

'Up yours,' retaliated Nathan. 'You don't get to tell me what to do. None of you get to do that. There was a time when kings and presidents hung on my every word, and now I have a Jamaican street thug telling me off. You're all a pathetic bunch of losers. Stuff you, Bastian,' shouted Nathan as he stormed off, slamming the door behind him.

'Man, talk about overreacting,' said Bastian. 'And that door slamming is beginning to become a bit of a habit as well.' He turned to look at Emily, holding his gaze on her for a full minute, until she began to feel really uncomfortable and looked away. 'How did you survive?' he asked.

Emily shrugged. 'Just lucky, I suppose.'

'One vamp, yep. Pretty sure you could

take one. Two, probably not. Maybe with a lot of luck. But four, no ways.'

'Well thanks for your total lack of confidence in me,' returned Emily.

'It's not that,' said Bastian. 'But Ambros just got hold of me. The cleanup team took the bodies to the manor house. Two of the vamps were real old. Well over six, seven hundred years. I can assure you; even I would have trouble taking out those two, let alone all four of them. So, how did you do it?'

Emily shrugged again.

'Come on, Emily. What aren't you telling? Seriously, talk to me.'

Haunting images of burning green eyes filled Emily's mind. And lips, red, kissable. *Damn it,* she thought as she cursed herself. *What the hell is wrong with me?*

Bastian was still staring at her. Awaiting an answer.

In desperation Emily said the first thing that came into her head. 'Umm – what is the *corona potestatem?*'

Bastian did a double take. 'What? Where did you hear that?'

'One of the vamps said it. He told me they were going to kill me to stop me looking for the *corona potestatem.* Which is a bit dumb because I don't even know what it is.'

The Jamaican sat down, took out a pack of cigarettes and lit one.

'Hey,' complained Emily. 'No smoking indoors. Anyway, I don't care what you say, those are bad for you. Coffin nails.'

Bastian's lips twitched up in a tiny smile. 'Come on, Em. I could drink battery acid and smoke crack cocaine and it wouldn't kill me. You know crap like that doesn't affect us.'

'Well it's still a gross habit. And…Em?'

Bastian shrugged. 'You don't like being called Em?'

Emily thought about it for a few seconds and then grinned. 'You know what? It's not bad. I've always been the full Emily but Em is fine. Anyway, this *corona potestatem* thing. Fess up, dude.'

'It's a myth. Doesn't exist.'

'Cool, so a bunch of blood suckers

want to kill me over something that doesn't exist. Come on Bastian.'

Bastian took a drag of his cigarette and blew a series of perfect smoke rings into the air. 'I'm not sure exactly what it's supposed to be. Some say it's a crown, some a ring. Whatever, the myth dates back many hundreds of years. The upshot of the whole thing is that this object, the *corona potestatem,* is meant to be able to give vampires the ability to walk in the daylight. It makes them immune to the sun. Not only that, it protects them against silver and, apparently, frees them from the need to drink human blood. Which means they would become pretty close to invincible.'

Emily shrugged. 'So? I mean if it only works on one vamp at a time, what's the big deal? We could still take him out, surely?'

'The big deal. Em, is that the only thing that stops a vamp being right at the top of the food chain is the fact that he has so many inherent weaknesses. Yin and yang. Balance. He has speed, strength, rejuvenation, immortality. Not to mention their capacity to glamour people into doing their bidding. But against them we have the power of light and silver. A vamp who is a daywalker is a big problem. I mean – he could become president of the United States if he wanted. Who could stop him? How could any normal human resist his glamour?'

Em nodded. 'Okay. So, this is bad then?'

'Yeah. But fortunately, we've all been searching for this so-called *corona potestatem* for hundreds of years now and Ambros is pretty convinced it doesn't exist. Or, if it ever did then it has been irretrievably lost. Still, if the vamps are seriously hot for it and they're willing to openly go to war over it then, regardless of whether it actually exists or not – it's a problem. I reckon we pack up and head back to the big house. We need to talk to Ambros and the rest of the troops.'

Em nodded her agreement.

Chapter 16

Ambros, Bastian and Emily sat in the old man's study. Nathan had stayed on in London, giving 'personal reasons' as his excuse not to return to the manor house.

'Sir William knows more than he's letting on,' said Ambros.

'I reckon that's true,' agreed Bastian. 'The vamps wouldn't randomly trash his place for no reason. They were looking for something he has. And it's ten to one he knows what it is.'

'No,' interjected Em. 'I spent an evening with him and I didn't get any hint he was hiding something.'

'I see,' said Ambros. 'So, you got to know him quite well then?'

'Well, no,' admitted Em. 'Not so much.' She thought for a while. 'To be honest, actually, he was pretty good at avoiding any questions about himself. He has a way of turning every question around so you end up talking about yourself all night.'

'So, what you're saying is, you didn't get to know him quite well then,' continued Ambros.

Em nodded. 'I suppose I didn't.'

'Can you get to see him again?' asked Ambros. 'I mean, socially, not in an official capacity.'

'Probably,' said Em. 'I've got his cell number; I could give him a call.'

'Do it now,' instructed the old man.

Emily left the room before she called, in order to have a little privacy and Ambros continued speaking to Bastian.

'This whole incident with Nathan,' said Ambros. 'The vamp attack and Emily managing to kill them all.'

'What about it?' asked Bastian.

'Give me your thoughts.'

The Jamaican shook his head. 'The first thing that springs to mind is – how the hell did the vamps know Emily and Nathan were there?'

'I agree. All I can think is that the vamps had someone following them. It's not exactly a secret that we own the St. Pancras flat.'

'True,' confirmed Bastian. 'Then, secondly, either Em is not telling us something or she's far better than I've given her credit for. I mean, two of the blood suckers were elders. Powerful. And the others were no Aspirants. I can't help thinking she couldn't have bested them all so easily. She hardly had a mark on her. Didn't ring true.'

'What did Nathan have to say?'

'Nothing. He said by the time he got there it was all over. Four headless blood vamps. Emily's sword had been blooded so, maybe it was her.'

'Logically, who could have helped her?' asked Ambros. 'Think about it. Unless they turned on each other. No human could have helped. They simply wouldn't have had the strength or speed to affect the outcome. *Id est*, it must have been her.'

'Occam's razor,' agreed Bastian. 'The simplest answer is usually the correct one. I suppose she got lucky. There is more,' he added. 'She said one of the vamps mentioned the *corona potestatem.*'

Ambros paled visibly and then he

leaned back in his chair and closed his eyes for a few seconds. 'Not again,' he whispered. 'I thought they had given up on that.'

'No real worries,' said Bastian. 'It doesn't actually exist, so they can search all they want. As long as they don't think we have it and start a war because of that. Actually,' he continued. 'I'd give good odds that the vamps were looking for it at Sir Williams place. Makes sense. More fools them.'

'Just because no one has found it for so long doesn't mean it doesn't exist,' countered Ambros. 'It simply means it hasn't been found. But even if it did there is no way it would simply be lying about in a random antique shop. That's just too ridiculous to countenance.'

'So, are you saying it does exist?' questioned Bastian.

Before Ambros could answer, Emily reentered the room, a smile on her face. 'Got hold of William. He's back at his estate in Kent. He invited me there to stay over for a night or two. I'm going to catch the train and his man will pick me up at the station.'

'We shall talk later,' said Ambros to the Jamaican, *sotto voce*. Then he turned to Emily. 'Good,' he affirmed. 'Now remember, this is not just a social visit. Find out what the hell is going on.'

Emily nodded. 'I'll do my best.'

Chapter 17

Head of the United Kingdom House of the *Nosferatu,* Lord Chelsea Byron, had long since lost the ability to feel remorse, or fear, or love. However, the last thousand years had honed his ambition to the point where it superseded all else. And so, even though he wasn't scared *per se,* he was nervous.

Because opposite him sat Janus Augusta, head of the Italian house and also the *Capo di tutt'i capi,* the supreme leader, of the entire World Vampire Federation.

Augusta had been born around 100BC and even for a vampire he was considered to be ancient. He sat in the leather wingback, his spine bent over almost double.

A network of throbbing purple veins stood out clearly on his hairless skull, as they did all over his body.

His fangs stood out on a permanent basis, at least four inches long and stained yellow with age. Uncut fingernails arched away from his fingers, so long that they literally curled back on themselves, preventing him from doing even the simplest of tasks for himself, a habit he affected to show that he had servants for everything.

But his eyes belied his frail appearance, Deep red in color and filled with a bottomless well of inhuman insanity. A pure madness brought on by living for far too long. A psychosis that can only come from having lost every friend, lover, and companion he had ever had. Thousands and thousands of years of bereavement and sorrow. A veritable litany of loss.

And with it came a hatred of all that was human.

When he spoke, his voice was so sibilant and quiet that, had his audience not had the hyper-sensitive hearing of the undead, they would not have been capable of hearing him.

'It is a shard of the true sword,' he said.

'After Sir Bedivere cast Excalibur into the lake, the Lady of the Lake, a succubus by the name of Nimue, destroyed the weapon, smashing it into pieces and flinging the shards into the deepest ocean.

But she retained one piece. A piece large enough to fashion a ring. This ring she gifted to Sir Lancelot. It was known as 'The Ring of Dispell' and it dispelled any enchantments. It is this ring that we seek. It is this artifact that shall give the *Nosferatu* wearer the power to become a Daywalker.'

'For many centuries we have searched for the relic,' said Lord Byron. 'How is it we have only now learned it is the fabled ring of Lancelot? Rumor has it as many different articles ranging from Solomon's crown to the Holy Grail.'

'Do you question me?' hissed Augusta.

Byron dropped to one knee before he replied. 'Never, my king. I merely enquire as to how we learned of its existence.'

'*We* did not,' replied the ancient vampire. '*I* did. And that is most likely due to the fact that I alone have been searching for it longer than anyone or anything on this earth.'

'A level one Familiar recently told us of rumors that pointed to a human, Sir William Townsend,' responded Byron. 'A dealer in antiquities. It was alleged he had come across a relic of great power. However, some of my Aspirants searched his premises and found nothing.'

'I have already heard about this,' interjected the *Capo di tutt'i capi.*

'Did the morons who work for you not think that any antiques shop of any value is bound to have many items with some sort of power in it?

We all know that age itself can bring power to an object. If we all merely romped about ransacking places with antiquities in, where would we be? I also heard they left evidence of their deed on camera for all to see. And now those infernal Shadowhunters are poking their filthy noses in our business.'

'That is true, my King,' agreed Byron. 'However, I did punish the Aspirants involved. I put two of them to the true death.'

Augusta sneered. 'You have grown soft, Lord Byron. See to it that the other Aspirants involved are also beheaded.'

Byron nodded. 'Of course, sire. It shall be done.'

'I know,' affirmed the ancient one. 'Now, tell me of your other blunders.'

'What blunders, my liege?'

The *Capo* hissed. 'Do not play with me, child,' he commanded. 'I know all. You insult me by performing parlor games. Four of your elder brethren have been killed. What happened?'

Byron flinched. He had thought that he had covered his tracks; however, once again, he had underestimated the leader's power and influence. 'There is a new Shadowhunter, my king,' he said. 'A mere child, only newly come into her powers. I sent four Enforcers to kill her, thinking that it might discourage the Foundation from looking any deeper into our affairs.'

'And what happened?'

'She killed them, sire.'

'How is that possible?' asked the ancient vampire.

Byron shook his head. 'Truly, I have no idea. Our informant assured us that, while she was talented, there was no way she could best four of our top exterminators. It is a mystery.'

'Did she receive help?' enquired Augusta.

'Our informant says not. Apparently, she did it herself.'

Augusta nodded. 'Interesting. Find out more about this new Hunter. Report back to me when you know everything about her. Lineage, history…everything.'

Lord Byron got off his knee and bowed deeply. 'As you command, so shall it be done.'

'Yes,' agreed Augusta. 'That is true. And I advise you never to forget that, Lord Byron. Now leave me, I grow hungry. Send me a Familiar. Someone young. Preferably male. A boy if you have.'

Byron bowed again and left the room.

Chapter 18

William's stately home, Taunton Abbey, was situated a couple of miles outside of the port town of Dover in Kent. His ancient driver had picked Emily up from Dover station and driven her to the residence. Truth be told, she was expecting a huge pile similar to the Foundation headquarters. But William's place was very different. A long, marble chip driveway led to a house that wasn't quite as large as the Foundation but was still magnificent. However, where Pankhurst Manor was all gargoyles and mullions, the Abbey was all light stone and glass. Hundreds of leaded windows reflected the sun and, instead of grotesques, the roof line was decorated with stone filigree, cherubs, and angels.

The only jarring point was a huge wolf's head carved above the main door, its jaws open wide, canines exposed and eyes staring madly ahead. Underneath, in Latin, *Vitae Passus Est.*

Em assumed it was the family motto. "Life is Suffering". She suppressed a shudder. The whole thing was incongruous when compared to the bright and beautiful surrounds.

The car pulled up in front of the sweeping steps that led to the front entrance, and the chauffeur clambered out, tottered around, and opened her door for her. Waiting at the top of the stairs stood William, his tousled hair a mess like he had just left it that way when he got out of bed that morning. But, as usual, the rest of him was immaculate. Olive moleskin trousers, Burman walking boots, a tan Orvis bush shirt and a sleeveless Shoffel shooting gilet in a dark chestnut.

He looked like a walking palette of autumnal shades.

He smiled, and Emily felt her heart leap. Then he strode down the stairs towards her and enveloped her in a huge hug. She could feel the heat of his body and it felt almost unbearably hot, as if he had a fever. His rangy muscles felt like steel hawsers as she pressed up against him. And his smell was masculine and comforting at the same time. A heady mixture of grass and ozone and leather and soap.

Then he suddenly pulled back and let his arms drop to his sides.

'Oh,' he exclaimed. 'I'm so sorry. What do you think of me? Manhandling you like that. I must apologize, it's just that, well, I was so pleased to see you. Got carried away, don't you know?'

Emily laughed. 'Don't be silly. I don't mind. Actually, it was nice; I'm also pleased to see you.'

William's smile returned two-fold as his obvious pleasure at her response painted itself across his face.

'Splendid,' he retorted. 'Awfully good. Well, the chaps will take the luggage up to your room. Chef has prepared us a light lunch, then perhaps I could take you on a little tour of the estate?'

Emily was pleased to see William's concept of a light lunch was so far off the mark as to be ludicrous. The table literally groaned under the weight of roast pheasant, slabs of home cured ham, stuffing, potatoes, and vegetables.

Ravenous as usual she piled her plate high and ate with gusto. William ate in the same fashion, consuming even more than Emily's Shadowhunter hungry metabolism and she wondered how he managed to stay in such good shape. With that calorific intake, she thought, he should be the size of Lyle. But she decided that discretion would be the better part of valor and deigned to ask him how he stayed so ripped when he ate enough to sustain four normal men.

True to his word, William showed her around the estate after lunch. She immediately fell in love with the place.

Rolling manicured lawns stretched for acres, leading down to the sudden drop of cliffs that overlooked the English Channel. To her right she could see the White Cliffs of Dover; resplendent in the cold English sun as they reflected the light off their unbelievably white surfaces.

Copses of oaks dotted the landscape and, scattered about the estate were random buildings that seemed to have no purpose other than decoration.

William called them Follies, and they ranged from the Beacon Tower, a fifty-five-foot-high tower, to the Faux castle, a huge façade of a medieval castle that stretched some five hundred feet from end to end, its purpose merely to improve the view from the main ballroom of the manor house.

'You don't have any livestock,' noted Emily as they walked about the estate.

'How do you mean?' asked William.

'No horses. No sheep, cows. I'd have expected livestock. I mean, I know it's not a farm, but I thought all English gentlemen had horses.'

William laughed. 'Well, not this one. Don't really like them and they can't stand me. Must be a family trait,' he continued. 'As far as I can remember, the Townsends have never ridden to the hounds or kept livestock or pets of any sort. Not even dogs.'

They wandered back to the house and William walked Emily through most of the formal rooms, withdrawing rooms, ballrooms, dining rooms. Each one more spectacular than the last.

Eventually Em started to experience a sort of luxury-overload. William picked up that she had seen about all that anyone could take in during one visit.

'Tell you what,' he said. 'I've got a few phone calls that I have to make before the market closes. Why don't I show you to the library, you can nose around there for a while and when you've had enough, pull one of the bell-cords and a chap will come and show you to your room? We'll be eating in tonight, so there's no need to dress but I'm sure that you shall want to avail yourself of the bathroom and such.'

Em smiled her agreement and, a few minutes later, she was alone in a magnificent library. She wandered around, not looking for anything specific, simply looking. She was surprised to find that, as well as many thousands of leather-bound musty old tomes, there were hundreds of more contemporary books. Ranging from Hemmingway through to Lee Child.

She picked a few up and thumbed through them. They were all first editions, and most had been signed and dedicated.

She picked up a first edition of The Picture of Dorian Gray by Oscar Wilde. It was dated 1890 and when she opened it she saw it was dedicated and signed by the great man himself. *To my Darling William*, it read. *Your munificence is overshadowed only by your compassion. Your friend forever, Oscar.*

Emily smiled to herself. Obviously, William's great-grandfather had been christened William as well.

Next, an original copy of Shakespeare's Macbeth caught her eye. *Man*, she said to herself. *This must be worth a pretty packet.*

Once again it was dedicated by the author. *William, remember always; 'He is mad that trusts in the tameness of a wolf'. With love and respect from your namesake, the other William.*

Em did a few figures in her head and worked out that all of the male Townsends for the last few hundred years must have all been called William. She raised an eyebrow. *Wow, family get togethers must have gotten confusing,* she mused.

She meandered down the room and eventually found herself in a low-ceilinged section. Here the books seemed older than all of the others. But despite their obvious age they were well preserved and, unlike many of the other books she had walked past, seemed so devoid of dust that they must have been fairly regularly used.

She ran her fingers along the shelf, reading the titles out to herself as she did.

The Book of Abramelin the Mage. The Ars Notoria.

Pseudomonarchia Daemonum. 'The false monarchy of demons,' translated Emily to herself. She took it down and flicked through it. The English was archaic and difficult to read but the book was basically a compendium from the 16th century, dictating the names of the sixty-nine major demons. *Weird,* she observed. *Wonder why he reads these?*

After a moment's thought, Em came to the conclusion that the books must be collectable as far as William's business was concerned and, with that minor mystery solved, she found the bell-cord and gave it a yank.

Shortly after that an old retainer arrived and showed her to her room.

Chapter 19

The evening meal had been fantastic and now Emily and William sat in the small withdrawing room. A fire crackled and spat in the massive fireplace and filled the area with a gorgeous mellow light.

William had poured a brace of liqueurs for the two of them. Something called Benedictine. The bottle looked hand blown and when Em looked at the label she could see the date of distillation, 1820. The drink was almost two hundred years old, she realized with a shock as she took a sip. The flavor was intriguing, unusual more than delicious.

'This bottle was made for me in the 18th century by a monk by the name of Francesco De Guilamme,' said William. 'From the Benedictine Abbey of Fecamp in Normandy. You can see here, on the label.' He pointed. 'The initials, DOM. Stands for *Deo Optimo*

Maximo.'

'To God, most good, most great,' translated Emily.

William smiled. 'Correct. So, you are a linguist as well as a jazz expert.'

Emily didn't react; she simply stared at the young man for a few seconds. Finally, she spoke. 'For you,' she said.

'What?' responded William.

'You said that the monk made it for you.'

'Did I?'

'Yes,' she affirmed. 'You did.'

'How silly of me,' said William. 'After all, that was over two hundred years ago.' He held the bottle up. 'Some more?'

Emily was about to refuse, but when she looked at her glass she saw she had finished her first tot, so she held out her glass for a refill.

'I saw some interesting books in your library,' she said. 'Particularly at the end of the room in that low-ceilinged area.'

'Ah, yes,' acknowledged William. 'The occult section.'

'Do you read any of those?'

'From time to time,' admitted William. 'Some of them are rather fascinating. Hard going though, mainly being in Latin.'

'Have you ever come across any mention of the *corona potestatem*?'

William frowned. 'The Crown of Power. I have read many stories, take your pick.'

'You tell me,' insisted Emily.

'The saying goes—He who wears the Crown of Power shall rule over all— but there is no definitive work saying what the Crown actually is. Many say it is merely the assumption of power, not an actual crown. Like the presidency or a potentate of some sort. Some say it was the crown of Aragon, others, that it was a ring worn by the Prince of Wallahia, Vlad the third. Or, as most people know him, Vlad the Impaler.'

Emily gasped. 'Dracula?'

'The same,' admitted William. 'Count Vladimir Dragwlya. Count Dracula.'

'The vampire.'

William laughed. 'Folklore and peasant superstition,' he said. 'There are no such things as vampires. Granted,

Vladimir was a complete psycho. Killed hundreds of thousands of people. Although, by all accounts his younger brother was quite a nice chap. He went by the moniker of Radu the Handsome.'

'Wow, no wonder Vlad was pissed,' noted Emily. 'His brother gets "Handsome" and Vlad gets "Impaler". I'd also be a little peeved.'

William laughed again. 'True, but it didn't make him a vampire. That was all due to the Irish author, Bram Stoker in 1897.

He didn't invent the vampire, but he definitely gave it its modern interpretation. He simply took Vlad's inherent evil and enhanced it by making him a vampire.'

'So, no *corona potestatem*?' asked Emily.

William shook his head. 'Afraid not. Still, that should help you sleep better at night. No vampires, no ghouls, and no monsters to disturb your slumber.'

The young sir walked Emily to her room. When they got there, he folded her into his arms, and hugged her tenderly. Then he kissed her on the lips. A soft, lingering kiss that rooted the Shadowhunter to the floor and threatened to take away her ability to stand on her own two legs.

And then he was gone.

Emily lay awake for ages, comfortable and warm but just on the edge of sleep. The full moon shone through the window and bathed all in a magical blue light that competed with the warm glow of the fire.

She got up off the bed and walked over to the window, staring out at the moon-drenched landscape. Ornamental bushes pruned into spheres and pyramids, a wide, stone pathway leading to an arboretum of mixed trees. Conifers, Willows and Oaks, their leaves and branches bleached to dark blues and grays by the moon's luminescence.

A sudden movement amongst the trees caught her eye.

A shadow loomed and then disappeared. She concentrated on the area, scanning from left to right, searching for another glimpse of whatever it was that had attracted her attention.

And then she saw it. A fleeting glance of no more than a fraction of a second as it moved through the trees, running with unbelievable speed and grace.

The largest wolf she had ever seen. Easily as tall as a horse.

Emily searched again but could see no further sign of it. And after a minute or more of fruitless staring, she began to doubt her own eyesight. The wolf, if indeed that was what it was, had been impossibly large. Surely it must have been a trick of the light. Probably a stray dog, or fox even. The moon had simply cast a large shadow that had rippled through the trees and made it look like a huge running wolf.

Yes, that must be it, she debated with herself.

She went back to bed and lay down. But, as the night wore on and before she found sleep, she knew deep down that what she had seen was no illusion.

Chapter 20

Lord Byron stared out of the window. The garden was lit by a gibbous moon and, to his immortal eyes it was as if it were the brightest summer's day. If he concentrated slightly he could hear the field mice scurrying though the long grass, the fox in his den and the soft whisper of a badger slipping through the brush.

Above he sensed an owl and, just for a moment, he melded his mind with that of the nighttime raptor and spent a few seconds looking at the earth from a height of over two hundred feet.

He could also smell the human that stood behind him.

He could hear the rushing of his blood, the breath hissing in and out of his lungs, the thud of his heartbeat. And from these physiological signs he could judge the human's emotions.

As always, he was surprised. There was

little or no fear there. Heart rate slightly elevated. Breathing normal. Stance comfortable but still respectful. Not relaxed but calm. The only emotion that came off the human in such strong waves it was almost a palpable thing, was its ambition. And its lust for power and respect.

He turned to face him.

'Young Nathan Tremblay,' he said. 'This is our third meeting yet still I struggle to fully accept your newfound loyalty to the *Nosferatu*. I ask myself, why would a Shadowhunter change ships in such a drastic fashion. Why would one throw away a hundred years of a chosen profession just like that?' He snapped his fingers to accentuate his point.

Nathan bowed his head in acknowledgement to the vampire's concerns. 'I understand, my lord,' he said. 'But you must know, being a Shadowhunter was never a chosen profession.

'I was born into it, much as a slave is born into his role in life. It was an assumption made by genetics.

However, it was never something I felt strongly about. What gives one faction the right to decide that another is evil? What makes the Olympus Foundation correct? It is mere semantics.

'And, for many years, I was relatively happy with my lot. As a Hunter we were revered. Respected amongst the upper echelons of government and high society. But those days have long passed. Nowadays to gain respect one has to be a reality television star, or a victim with a story of abuse and exploitation. A woman giving birth to her child on national television, or a mediocre singer with a sorry childhood. Talent has become a misnomer and fame has taken the place of true worth. And for this we are expected to lay down our lives? Truth be told, my lord, modern society sickens me. Humanity needs to be controlled and who better to do that than the *Nosferatu?*'

'So, my child,' said Byron. 'You seek power?'

'I have made no secret of that, my lord,' agreed Nathan.

Byron stood silent for a while. 'You

have shown your loyalty, I suppose,' he conceded. 'You did help to set up the destruction of your colleague, Miss Hawk. However, you blundered by hopelessly underestimating her capabilities and that mistake cost the lives of four of our brethren.'

'And for that I am most distressed, my lord. I had no idea she was so proficient.'

'Even more reason that she must be taken out,' said Byron.

'Yes, sire,' agreed Nathan. 'And as I have informed you, she is now with the English nobleman, Sir William. This time the team you are sending to assure her demise will be successful. No single being could stand against ten brethren; even if some of them are mere Grinders.'

Byron smirked. 'Do not underestimate the raw strength of the Grinders,' he advised. 'They may be simple, but their power and dedication are nothing to be sneered at.'

'I meant no offense, master,' assured Nathan. 'I am also confident the rest of the members of the Foundation shall see their lives end tonight,' he continued. 'I have given the Enforcer the codes to the doors and gates of Pankhurst Manor as well as the whereabouts of the cameras and alarms. The team he is sending there will definitely take the Shadowhunters by complete surprise. Their end is indeed nigh.'

Again, the Lord Byron stood silent. Contemplating.

Finally, he spoke. 'Yes,' he said. 'I have decided. You have proved your faithfulness and devotion to the brethren, beyond any doubt. The ceremony shall take place tonight. While the Enforcer teams are out destroying the Olympus Foundation, we shall be creating a fresh life for our newest member. Our first ex-Shadowhunter. The *Nosferatu* Nathan Tremblay.'

And Nathan fell to his knees in supplication to his new master.

Chapter 21

Emily and William had taken an early dinner and now, once again, Em was walking through the endless rooms of the manor house. Exploring while William made his nighttime calls to the various markets around the world.

This time she found herself in yet another massive reception room, the walls filled with large oil paintings of the Townsend men throughout the ages. And every one of them looked remarkably like William. Or, she supposed, to be more accurate, he looked like them.

She was looking at one portrait in particular. Major William Townsend circa 1815. Dressed in a scarlet, long tailcoat with a gold star on each shoulder. Tight fitting white tights, long black boots, a saber, a flintlock and a bicorne hat. The resemblance was uncanny, right down to the shy smile and the muscular build.

As Emily was staring, one of the ancient retainers walked by the open door, she peered in and smiled, an almost toothless grin.

'Good evening, young miss,' she said. 'I see you are admiring the paintings of the master.'

'Yes,' smiled Emily. 'I must say, the family resemblance is remarkable.'

The old lady looked puzzled. 'I'm not sure I understand, my lady. The master has always looked like that. As you can see in that one there,' she pointed at the painting of the major. 'That's always been one of my favorites. That was done just after he returned from the war after giving that Napoleon chap a good drubbing.'

Emily raised an eyebrow. 'I'm sorry, what are you saying?'

'The master,' repeated the old servant. 'He's looked just like that for as long as I can remember, and I've been in his service for over seventy years now.'

Emily did a double take. 'But that's impossible,' she said, her face pale with shock.

'Oh dear,' wailed the old lady. 'You didn't know. Oh dear…it's not my fault,' she cried. 'The master didn't warn us. He should have told. Oh, that naughty man.'

Right then William walked in. He took a look at Emily's face and then old lady and he sighed.

'I'm so sorry, master,' wailed the old girl. 'You didn't tell us that she didn't know.'

William smiled. 'Don't worry, Winifred, I'll take care of this. You go make sure that Emily's fire in her bedroom is lit.'

Winifred bowed, shuffled off, and closed the door as she left, her face a picture of contrition.

Emily's expression, on the other hand, was a combination of righteous anger and disappointment.

'Right,' she said, her voice husky with emotion. 'You had better do some bloody quick explaining Sir William, or whatever your name is. And this had better be good.'

'Look, Emily,' stated William. 'It's not

what you think.'

'How do you know?' shouted Emily. 'How could you possibly know because you don't know what I'm thinking you…?' She searched for a suitable word. 'You – bumhole.'

William stopped mid-flow and raised an eyebrow. 'Really? Bumhole?'

Emily shrugged. 'I'm not good with swear words,' she admitted.

'But, bumhole,' repeated William. 'It's so juvenile.'

'Oh, I'm so sorry,' quipped Emily. 'We can't all be twenty thousand years old,' she pointed at the paintings as she answered. 'We can't all have been alive since the bloody dinosaurs. Some of us are just infantile, immature babies who've only been alive for eighteen years.' She stamped her foot. 'You shit head.'

William nodded. 'Well, okay. As far as cursing goes, that one was a little better. Listen, my dearest,' he continued. 'I promise I can explain. But first there are a few things I need to show you.'

He held out his hand and waited for

Emily to take it.

After a few seconds she shook her head. 'No holding hands,' she said. 'First you explain. And then I decide if I ever want to talk to you again. Ever.'

'Right,' conceded William. He rolled his head on his neck, took a deep breath to prepare. And then he stopped and stood stock still, head tilted to one side, eyes squinted in concentration.

'What?' asked Emily. 'What's wrong?'

Without answering William sniffed the air like a dog, moving his head from side to side as he did so.

'Okay,' stated Emily. 'This is getting creepy. What the hell is going on?'

'Dammit,' growled William. 'What the hell are they doing here?' He turned to face Emily. 'Look, we're going to have to talk about this later. We have a big problem. Quickly, you need to hide.'

'Wait,' demanded Emily. 'Who is here? You had better tell me what the hell is going on or I'm not going anywhere. And don't think you can get out of an explanation by simply coming over all weirdo on me.'

William grabbed her by the arm. 'I'm

sorry, Em,' he said. 'But it's for your own safety.' He started to walk off, pulling her by the arm. But instead, Emily pulled back, lifting him off his feet and yanking him back towards her.

He looked at her with an astonished expression on his face. 'What the...? That's impossible. No one that size can be that strong.'

'Well obviously that assumption isn't correct,' snapped Emily. 'So, I advise you to start doing some explaining and quickly.'

William shook his head. 'I'm sorry, my darling,' he said sadly. 'But it's too late.'

As he spoke the door burst open.

Ten vampires stalked into the room, their fangs already extended, lips pulled back and claws bared.

Emily sprinted to the wall and pulled off a saber that was mounted next to one of the paintings. She ran her thumb along the blade and was pleased to see it was still sharp.

'Get behind me,' she shouted at William as she moved towards the blood suckers.

The group of vamps laughed as they fanned out and advanced on her, hissing and screeching.

Then next to her she heard a tremendous roar and the vamps pulled back in surprise. Emily turned to look at the source of the savage noise to see William tearing his shirt off as he rapidly swelled in size. Hair started to sprout from his body and, as she watched, his face elongated, growing a muzzle and fangs.

He fell to all fours as the final remnants of his clothing were rent from him.

And suddenly there was no longer William. Instead, there stood a wolf the size of a horse.

He threw back his head and howled. The sound affected Emily on a visceral level. An atavistic call of the wild.

Without warning, the wolf sprang forward and, moving with unbelievable grace and speed, he attacked the vampires. He landed on top of the leading vamp and, with a savage wrench, tore the creature's head off with one blood drenching bite.

Using the vampires' confusion, Emily

leapt into the fray, brandishing the blade with all of her Shadowhunter enhanced strength. The old blade wasn't silver-coated, but it could still chop heads off, if wielded with enough power. And Emily was possessed of that power.

She lopped off a blood sucker's head and then spun onwards, moving all of the time.

Striking and cutting without pause or conscious thought as she moved in perfect tandem with the Wolf. Together they danced an intricate ballet of death and dismemberment.

In the periphery of her vision, Emily noticed two elderly male servants enter the room carrying large crossbows. She heard the thump of the bows being discharged and two vampires fell screaming to the floor. Emily realized the bolts must be silver impregnated and, taking advantage of the blood suckers' agony; she chopped down at them, removing their heads with two mighty blows.

She spun again, searching for her next victim.

But the attack was over. Dismembered and decapitated bodies lay strewn around the room. Blood ran down the walls and dripped from the ceiling.

And standing in the middle of the room was the wolf that used to be William.

That still was William.

Emily dropped the sword and walked slowly up to the animal. The wolf looked back at her with William's eyes. She went right up to him and threw her arms around his neck.

The wolf pushed back at her with his head, growling softly as he did so.

Then he pulled back and started to shift. His fur receded. He shrank down to his former size. And there he stood. In front of her.

Naked.

Emily ran her gaze over him. The broad muscles of his chest, the bulging shoulders and biceps. The chiseled abs. And lower… she blushed.

William grinned, winked, and left the room.

As he walked past the two servants they dropped to one knee, their heads held downwards in respect.

Emily followed him.

Chapter 22

A single black candle guttered in the corner, the shaky orange flame seeming somehow to enhance the darkness rather than do anything to alleviate it. On a marble slab lay a naked body. Arms by its sides, hair greased back into a short ponytail. In a circle around the altar stood six elder vampires. The elite of the United Kingdom chapter of the *Nosferatu*.

Lord Byron stepped forward and approached the body.

Then with shocking savagery and a total lack of ceremony he bit into its neck. The person on the slab screamed out in agony as blood pumped from the jagged wound, flowing down his chest and arms and legs.

With a final shake of his head, Lord Byron tore a chunk of flesh from the victim and then stood back, once more a part of the circle of elders.

The body jerked spasmodically a few times, heels drumming against the marble once, twice, thrice. Then a death rattle gurgled from its ruined throat and it lay still.

Dead.

'Will he reanimate?' asked Cromwell the Enforcer. 'And if so, will he become a Grinder?'

'He will reanimate,' confirmed Lord Byron. 'I could taste his power. You see, Enforcer, he is already very old. And, strictly speaking, he is not even human. I have a feeling he will be a great asset to our chapter and to our movement.'

'I still wonder if he can he be trusted?' questioned the Enforcer.

'Oh yes,' answered the lord. 'He is sick of playing the underdog. He yearns for the power and influence that he once had. And the lust for power is a far stronger drive than either love or hate. Believe me, he will become one of our greatest resources. Already he has shown his loyalty and dedication. And, thanks in part to him, by the end of this day we will be stronger than ever before. We shall be almost unchallenged. An unstoppable force.'

There was a scream and a howl as the dead body twitched into animation and the new aspirant stood up.

He glanced around at the circle of elders and he smiled, his fangs sliding out like two ivory daggers, his neck wound already healed into a ragged pink scar.

'Incredible,' breathed Lord Byron. 'Instead of taking hours to heal and change he literally took a matter of minutes.'

The new Aspirant walked over and knelt before the lord. 'My lord. I am your servant.'

Lord Byron nodded. 'And it is with love and honor that I accept you into the house of Byron. Stand, Nathan Tremblay, former Shadowhunter, and take your place at my side.'

Chapter 23

The Bentley Continental GT8 belted along at over one hundred miles an hour. It was still nighttime. After the vamp attack, Emily and William had cleaned themselves up. Then Emily tried to contact Ambros to tell him about the attack. But she was unable get hold of anyone. The landline to Pankhurst Manor was down and no one answered their cell phones.

William agreed with Emily that they should proceed to Pankhurst as quickly as possible.

'You lied to me,' snapped Emily.

'No,' refuted William. 'Well, perhaps, but only thorough omission. Never an outright lie. I would never do that to you. Ever.'

'So, when were you going to tell me then?' insisted Em. 'At what stage of our relationship were you going to inform me that you were a werewolf?'

William smiled. 'We have a relationship? Splendid.'

'Oh, shut it. I'm really angry with you,' yelled Emily.

'Well what about you?' asked William. 'When were you going to tell me that you were Buffy the vampire slayer? And, by the way, I'm not a werewolf.'

'Please William. I bloody saw you turn onto a wolf the size of a trailer home.'

'Yes, granted. But I'm still not a werewolf. Technically, I'm a shape-shifter.'

'Tomato – tomahtoh.'

'No. It's a very different thing,' insisted William. 'Believe me, I know quite a few werewolves. They have to change during a full moon. It's a biological imperative. And when they do, they have very little control over their animal instincts. They hunt. And that is pretty much what dominates their thoughts. They can also change at will during other phases of the moon and at those times they are more in charge of their faculties.'

'And you?' asked Emily. 'What's the big difference?'

'The change is never forced upon me, no matter what the moon is doing. Also, I'm bigger, much bigger, faster, and stronger than your common and garden werewolf, although I am still vulnerable to silver. But probably the biggest difference is that, as a shifter, I control the level of the change. If I want, I can half change or even less. Sort of an upright man come wolf hybrid. So, I have the enhanced strength, speed and healing but can still walk upright and talk. After a fashion, anyway. Werewolves are pretty much an all-or-nothing state. Man, or wolf.'

'I get it,' admitted Em. 'A month ago, I would have freaked out big time but now, well, I won't say that being attacked by vampires and being defended by a werewolf...'

'Shape-shifter,' interrupted William.

'Whatever, I won't say it's meh...but it's in the realms of normal. So, what's your excuse for denying that Vamps exist?'

'I was protecting you. How was I to know you were a Shadowhunter?'

'True,' admitted Em. 'So, you know

about Shadowhunters then?'

'I'm hundreds of years old and I'm a shape-shifter. Of course I know about the Olympus Foundation, in fact I have had many dealings with them in the past. Just not recently. Well, not for many years, actually.'

'I'm only eighteen and a few weeks ago I considered that to be a young adult. Now that I'm surrounded by all of these thousand-year-old men I'm starting to feel like a bit of a baby.'

'Steady. Hundreds...not thousands.'

'Whatever.'

'Anyway,' continued William. 'It doesn't work like that. Physical age has nothing to do with how old or knowledgeable or experienced you are. It's a spiritual thing. As a Shadowhunter you come from a long line of selectively bred superhumans. Their memories, their experiences... they are all inside you. Just waiting to be unlocked. Your physical being is eighteen years old, but your essence is many hundreds if not thousands of years old. Particularly if both of your parents are of the original line.'

'They are,' confirmed Emily.

'Well then, Emily Shadowhunter Hawk. You are a very special person.'

'Cool, Thanks. How much longer until we get to the manor? I'm seriously worried about them.'

'Not long. But I wouldn't worry. There's no way that anything bad could happen to a group of Shadowhunters. I mean, it would take a full-scale war to bring harm to them, a concentrated attack by sixty plus vamps, maybe more if you include the grinders. And I don't see the brethren launching a war for no reason.'

'Maybe they have a reason,' says Em.

'What?' asked William.

'What I already told you.'

William drew a deep breath. 'The *corona potestatem* Is that why you mentioned it? Are they looking for it?'

'Apparently,' confirmed Emily. 'I ran into a few of them a couple of days back and they brought the subject up. But why should that matter? You've already told me it doesn't exist.'

William grimaced. 'I may have been a little light with the truth there.'

'Oh, big surprise. Don't tell me, you lied again. Is anything that you've actually told me the truth?'

'Everything is true,' reacted William. 'Except for the shape-shifter thing. And the vamps. Oh, and the *corona potestatem*. It does exist but that is all I can tell you.'

'That's all you know?'

William shook his head. 'I'm not going to lie to you again, Emily. I know much more about it but I'm not at liberty to tell you. I've sworn a blood oath and I cannot break it.'

Emily sat back in her seat with a sigh and kept silent.

Meanwhile, William drove the massive sports saloon like it was an extension of his own body, taking impossibly narrow gaps and barreling around corners on two wheels. They got to the gates of the manor house in record time only to find them wide open.

William raced up the driveway, turning his beams off as he did.

'Let's not telegraph our arrival,' he explained. 'Just in case.'

'Hey,' said Emily. 'You do know it's

nighttime? People need light to see.'

William smiled tightly. 'I see just as well at night.'

Em shrugged. 'So do I, I guess it's just habit to want lights on.'

As they drew closer to the house William shook his head. 'I don't like this. Something's wrong. No lights. And look,' he said as he brought the car to a halt. 'The front door has been smashed off its hinges.'

He opened the car door and then ran around to the trunk and pulled out a katana in a scabbard. He handed it to Emily. 'This sword has been in our family for centuries. It was crafted by Japan's greatest swordsmith, Goro Masamune, over seven hundred years ago. Its blade has been coated with silver. Now, it is yours.'

Emily accepted the sword and belted the scabbard around her waist.

William took out another item and handed it to her. 'Colt .45,' he said. 'Para-ordnance frame, so it holds fifteen rounds. Silver-tipped bullets.'

Emily stuck the pistol into her belt with a nod of thanks.

William started to strip, throwing his clothes into the trunk as he did so.

'Hey, what're you doing?' asked Em.

'I'm going to change,' he answered. 'No need to ruin another set of clothes, so I'll take them off first.'

'Oh, of course,' acknowledged Emily. She half looked away but not so much that she couldn't still see him. As William pulled off his boxers he glanced at her, caught her eye, and winked. She blushed and straightaway cursed herself for not being able to control her autonomic response, as Bastian put it.

But she continued to peek as William changed. This time he didn't go full-wolf but sort of metamorphosed into a man-wolf hybrid. At the end of the transformation he stood almost eight feet tall and the muscles on his arms, chest and legs were monstrous, like someone had constructed him out of raw concrete. A thick layer of dark fur covered his body. And his face, although undeniably still William, developed a protruding snout, large exposed canines, and pointed ears.

'Let's go,' he growled, his voice a savage blend of animal and human.

Emily followed the Wolfman up the stairs to the broken front door. Just before they went inside William held his paw up. 'Wait,' he said in a soft growl. 'I smell blood. Humans and vampire. Also, something else.' He sniffed the air. 'Zombies?' he questioned.

Emily nodded. 'The servants were zombies,' she affirmed.

The wolf-man shook his head. 'That's grotesque.'

'It's not what you think,' defended Emily.

'Whatever,' responded William. 'Let's proceed with caution.'

Emily followed him into the manor, drawing her sword as she did so. They moved silently, all senses alert.

They walked down the long corridor on the ground floor, William leading the way, allowing his sense of smell to guide him.

Slowly, he pushed the door of the drawing room open. Emily gasped in shock as they walked in. The carpets were soaked with blood. There were also large splashes of it on the walls and even the ceiling. Scattered around the room were three headless vamp bodies and, in the far corner, the diminutive corpse of Josephine Brady. Her katana was broken, the blade snapped in two. In her hand was a Glock 10mm pistol, the slide racked back, showing it was empty. Emily checked Josephine's pulse, but it was obvious by the gaping wounds in her chest and neck, that she was dead.

They left the room and ghosted back along the corridor checking the other rooms as they did so. In the kitchen they discovered another two dead vampires, their heads had been torn from their shoulders with great force and around them lay the bodies of five of the zombie servants, their arms and legs ripped off, massive gaping holes in their torsos. But no blood. Like dismembered dolls. Broken puppets.

'Zombies are incredibly strong,' noted William. 'But slow. They managed to get a couple of the blood suckers though. Good on them.' He looked closely at the vampire remains. 'Grinders,' he said. 'Not true vampires. Look,' he pointed. 'Misshapen heads, slightly malformed bodies. Strong and quick but stupider than a box of horse shoes. Fanatically obedient to their masters. The Vamps use them as cannon fodder.'

Again, they wandered through the charnel house of death, seeking Emily's friends. As they got close to the dining room William held up his hand.

'I can smell fresh blood in there,' he said. Emily stood behind him as he placed his massive paw on the door. Then, with a huge surge of power, he simply smashed it off its hinges and charged into the room.

This time, the sight of seven dead vamps greeted them, four of them grinders. And, lying on the table, Karl's dead body. All about him were spent shell casings and in each hand, he held a Desert Eagle pistol. His throat had been torn open and it was obvious something had fed on him, as there were bite marks on his arms and face. 'The Grinders did that,' said William.

'They often feed on their victims. And not just blood, they eat the flesh'

He tilted his head to one side and then, without warning, he ran from the room and Emily followed.

They twisted and turned down corridors until William crashed through a set of double doors into a huge ballroom. In the middle of the room stood two men.

And surrounding them were close on twenty vampires. A mix of Grinders, Adepts, and Masters. The Grinders were gibbering like hyenas, jumping up and down with bloodlust and excitement, whilst the other blood suckers were hissing and howling as they attacked.

Emily saw that it was Piet and Lyle who were facing off against the pack. Both were bleeding from multiple wounds. Piet was wielding his katana and a short dagger while Lyle had a massive war hammer in his hands. On the floor were the dead and wounded bodies of at least another twelve vampires. The place was a nightmare of blood and gore. Hieronymus Bosch's version of hell.

William instantly slipped into full wolf mode, dropping to all fours, and attacking, tearing into the exposed vampires' backs.

Emily drew her pistol and started firing off rounds. Her shots landed true but although they put a few vamps down, she knew that the hits wouldn't kill them. At that moment, however, she was simply happy to slow them down some.

The slide racked back. Empty. She launched herself at the vamps, drawing her katana, and striking in one fluid movement. Once again the room became a stage for the dance of death and destruction.

Vamps screamed, William howled his hatred, and Piet and Lyle cried out in anger and physical effort.

The first Shadowhunter to go down was Lyle, as even his great strength could not keep the multitude of vampires at bay. Blood poured from a huge number of wounds and he was borne to the floor by a pile of Grinders who slashed and bit at him, ripping open his jugular and painting themselves with his blood. As they started to feed on him, Piet roared and attacked, hacking them off Lyle's body.

'Get up, fat man,' he shouted. 'We're not done yet.'

But there was no answer and before Piet could turn, a Master jumped him from behind and bit down on the back of his neck. Piet fell to the floor twitching in agony as he did.

Emily and William were forced into the corner as the remaining dozen blood suckers fanned out and readied themselves to attack.

William glanced at Emily and, even though he could not talk in full wolf mode, his expression was easy to read. His devastation at not being able to protect her. His helplessness. His feelings of despair.

Emily smiled. 'Hey,' she said. 'There's only a few of them. Tell you what, I'll take the ones on the left and you take the ones on the right.'

William gave her a wolfy grin, exposing his four-inch-long canines.

But just before they launched

themselves at the approaching blood suckers, something came crashing through the floor-to-ceiling windows that lined the one side of the ballroom.

A single man in a black cloak, spinning in the air as he leapt in.

Emily looked up. His cloak billowed about him as he landed, His long black hair hung down past his shoulders and his pale face was unshaven. His lips, full and sensual and as red as blood. His skin as pale as an angel of the grave. With a flourish he drew his rapier and attacked.

William and Emily followed suit, hacking, tearing, and carving their way through the surprised brood of vampires.

Within seconds all of the brethren lay dead. William prowled around the room, checking to make sure, using his massive jaws to tear the heads from the shoulders of anyone he suspected might still be alive.

Then he changed back to his Wolfman mode, while Emily rushed over to check on Piet.

Meanwhile, the newcomer stood still,

about fifteen feet away, his rapier by his side. Silent. Alert but not nervous.

'You,' growled William.

The newcomer bowed theatrically. 'Yes, Sir William. It is I, Sylvian Baptiste at your service.'

'You two take care of Emily,' grunted Piet. 'Also, I don't know where Bastian or Nathan is. Ambros was here but he disappeared.'

'What do you mean?' asked Emily. 'He ran away?'

'No,' said Piet. 'In the middle of the fight he got bitten bad and then he just disappeared. Poof. Gone.' The big man grimaced in pain. 'Oh, man,' he gasped. 'This bloody hurts. Do me a favor, Emily,' he continued. 'Do you think you could get me something to drink? I mean alcoholic. Brandy maybe.'

'Of course,' said Emily. 'Just lie still.'

She stood up and as she was looking around the ballroom to check if there was a drinks cabinet of some sort, a shockingly loud gunshot echoed through the room. She looked back at Piet to see that he had drawn a pistol, put it to his temple and pulled the trigger.

'Oh no,' she cried out as she knelt next to him. 'Why?'

'He is a brave man,' said William. 'He didn't want to turn so he killed himself before he could. Come now, let us check the rest of the house for survivors.'

Emily shook her head. 'There is no one else,' she whispered as tears rolled down her cheeks

'What are your plans?' asked Sylvian.

Emily looked up at him for a few seconds, her mouth open but mute.

'She didn't survive the change, but the bite brought on labor. So, alas, I was born to a dead mother. As such, it is true that I have many traits of the vampire. I am not immortal, but I do live an extended life. Like the blood suckers I cannot take daylight, so have to live at night. However, I don't have to drink human blood to survive. I eat normal foods, although I do have fangs, but I use them only for battle. Obviously, I also have increased strength and speed and eyesight. So,' he ended. 'Not a vampire but almost a vampire. *Tu comprends*?'

Emily nodded.

'And so,' continued Sylvian. 'That is why I hunt the vampire. They killed my mother and they cursed me to live forever in the dark,' he spat on the floor. *'Merde!'*

'So, you saving me was simply a by-product of your hunt?' asked Emily.

Again, Sylvian did the French shrug. 'Perhaps.

But still it is a happy coincidence is it not?'

'Emily,' interrupted William, still in Wolfman mode. 'We need to get out of here. Do you have anything you need to collect?'

Emily put her hand to her pendant that Ryoko had gifted her only a few weeks and also a lifetime ago. She shook her head. 'I have everything I need,' she said

'Clothes,' said William. Emily took a deep breath.

All that she wanted to do was leave but William was right. She needed clothes.

William nodded at Sylvian and then

glanced at Lyle's body. An unspoken request flashed between them and the Frenchman nodded and drew his rapier, knowing that Sir William wanted him to ensure that none of the dead Shadowhunters could turn. Sylvian would remove their heads when Emily was out of the room.

Then the Wolfman followed Emily to her room where she grabbed a rucksack and piled all of her black Shadowhunter outfits in. She didn't bother with her dresses as she figured that the time for frivolities was over, although she still retained enough vanity to pack her new makeup and beauty products. 'Right,' she said. 'Let's get the hell out of this slaughterhouse.'

The three of them ran from the house. William opened the trunk to retrieve his clothes, morphing back as he did so. After quickly pulling on his outfit he jumped into the driver's seat. Emily climbed into the back seat and Sylvian rode shotgun. The powerful engine roared and the car sped down the driveway.

'I'm going to head to London,' said

William. 'That alright with you?' he questioned Sylvian.

'Oui,' confirmed the bloodborn. 'If you are heading for your London home then you go close to Sloane Square. Please drop me there.'

'Why?' enquired William.

'It is where I dwell at the moment. In the Holy Trinity Church opposite Sloane Square. The priest there is a friend.'

'Understanding priest to allow a vampire in the house of god.'

'Up yours, William,' said Sylvian. 'After a few hundred years that joke is wearing a bit thin.'

'I disagree,' chuckled William. 'Still makes me laugh.'

'Yes. But you have a very basic sense of humor. Anyway, the priest isn't human. He's a Cluracan.'

'A what?' asked Emily.

'Cluracan,' answered William. 'Sort of an Irish leprechaun. Except normal sized. Kind souls and always willing to help a lost cause. Unusual to find one working as a priest though.'

'He was cast out of the underground

kingdom last century,' said Sylvian. 'Ended up in the church. Does a good job actually.'

Emily shook her head. 'Just when I think I'm getting to grips with things, you guys spring something else on me. I mean, is anyone a normal human or are we surrounded by the occult and weirdo types?'

Both William and Sylvian laughed out loud. 'Actually,' said Sylvian. 'There are a surprising number of the fey folk present in human society. Wizards, werewolves, vampires, leprechauns, ghouls, banshees, demons, kobolds, jotnar. The list goes on and on.'

'What about elves and hobbits?' asked Em.

'Oh, be serious,' quipped Sylvian. 'This isn't Lord of the Rings, this is real life.'

'Oh, excuse me,' countered Emily and she stuck her tongue out at the bloodborn count.

'Charming,' mumbled Sylvian. 'Uh, here.' Then he said to William. 'Drop me off, it's close enough and I need to move. It's only twenty-seven minutes to sunrise.'

'You know the exact time the sun is going to come up?' questioned Emily.

'Of course,' answered Sylvian. 'Life and death knowledge.'

William pulled the car over to the side of the road and Sylvian got out. He turned, waved, and then simply seemed to disappear as he moved so fast. William pulled off again.

'He seems nice,' noted Emily.

'He's a pompous French ass,' quipped William. 'Oh. And you?' teased Em.

'I'm entirely different,' argued William. 'I'm a pompous English ass.'

He slowed down and stopped outside a massive townhouse. Then he pressed a remote control on his visor and the automatic gate slid open in front of them.

The house was situated in Kensington Palace Gardens road, opposite the Nepalese embassy and, although Emily was unaware of the fact, if purchased in the current market it would have set the new owner back more than thirty million dollars.

William steered the car down a ramp

into an underground parking lot and then Emily followed him up a flight of steps and into the entrance hall.

An old servant waited for them at the top of the stairs, greeting William with a nod of and a quiet, 'Sir.'

'Good evening, Halston,' answered William. 'This is Emily, she shall be staying in the blue room tonight. Wake chef and tell him to prepare a meal. Something quick and substantial. A good fry up will do nicely.'

The servant nodded again and went off to do Sir William's bidding.

'Come along,' said William. 'I'll show you to your room. You can have a quick shower, change, whatever, and then ring the bell and someone will come and show you to the dining room.'

Emily did as William suggested and half an hour later they were chowing down on platters of fried eggs, bacon, sausages, baked beans, mushrooms, kidneys, black pudding and toast.

As they ate, William talked. 'We have a problem,' he stated.

'No shit, Sherlock,' responded Emily.

'All my friends are dead, well, except for Nathan and Bastian and no one knows where they are.'

'It's worse than that,' said William. 'It's obvious that the brethren are looking to completely wipe out the Olympus Foundation.

I'm not sure why they chose now to do it, but I suspect it might have something to do with the whole *corona potestatem.*'

'Well then they've pretty much done what they set out to do,' exclaimed Emily.

'Not true,' argued William. 'Three of you are left and we're not sure what happened to your wizard chap. Also, there are Olympus members all over the world. We need to find them. It's a great pity you're so new to the whole thing, a bit more knowledge of the structure of the Foundation would be invaluable.'

'I know the passwords to get into the computer records. They're in the cloud. There must be some info there.'

'Good,' affirmed William. 'But for now, we need to address the biggest problem. You.'

'Me?'

'Yes. The vamps are going to keep coming after you. They've tried twice already and, as far as they're concerned, you have single-handedly defeated all comers. By now they will be convinced that you are superman and the terminator rolled onto one. The next time they come it will be in numbers that will certainly overwhelm us. Even if Sylvian is present.'

Emily frowned. 'What do we do?'

'Well, you've got to go off-grid somehow. It's no good staying here. My London residence is no secret. Also, I'm sure that by tomorrow they'll have some Familiars watching me around the clock.'

'Where can I go?' asked Emily.

'I have a number of apartments that are registered in the names of certain trusts,' answered William. 'Totally untraceable back to me. I'll give you the keys to one of them. Can you ride a motorcycle?'

Emily nodded. 'Sure.'

'Right. I've got a Harley Davidson V-

Rod you can have. It's also registered to an offshore trust. Better than a car, faster in traffic. Also, you'll need some more ammunition for the Glock, maybe a couple more firearms.'

Emily shook her head. 'I don't want to go.'

William took her hand and kissed it. 'You sort of have to,' he said softly. 'You've got a target painted on you and you've got a bunch of blood suckers looking to fire at it. Staying with me will only make things worse. Look, I'm also going to give you a handful of burner phones. I'll pre-program the corresponding numbers into each one. You can phone me whenever you need to and then destroy the phone afterwards. Come on, let's get you kitted.'

It took William less than an hour to sort Emily out. She had her clothes, half a dozen throwaway cell phones, one hundred rounds of ammunition with three extra magazines for the Glock, her katana, a sawn-off double-barrel shotgun with a pistol grip, short enough to conceal under her jacket, extra ammo for the same. A selection of throwing knives and a thick wad of cash in various denominations adding up to twenty thousand Pounds Sterling. And her makeup.

The Harley was a beauty. Matt black with a larger gas tank for extended mileage and a SatNav. William punched the address of the apartment into the SatNav and handed Emily the keys.

There was no need to postpone the inevitable.

They stared at each other. Emily desperately wanted to kiss him. To hold him tight and run her hands down his chest and over his taut abs and more. But she knew that, if she did, she wouldn't have the strength to leave. As it was she felt like she was tearing her own heart out.

So instead she simply donned her helmet, started the Harley, and rode out.

And into the next phase of her life.

Chapter 24

It had been two weeks since the Pyrrhic victory over the Olympus Foundation. Lord Byron could still feel the pain of his dying brethren. Of course not the Grinders. They were mere animated meat bombs. Weapons of violence to unleash and use up. But, apart from the thirty or so Grinders, the true death had been brought upon fifteen brethren. And of those, three were Elders. In one night, the United Kingdom Chapter had lost over five thousand years of collective experience.

An insufferable loss.

But at the same time, they had gained something unique. Something no one had ever encountered before. They had turned a Shadowhunter.

Standing before him was the result. And it was magnificent.

Nathan Tremblay stood, legs slightly apart, his shirtless torso showing off an almost impossibly ripped musculature. His stance was relaxed and in his right hand he held a sword. On his face, there was a slight smile.

No, thought Byron to himself. Not a smile. A sneer. Of contempt.

Four other vampires surrounded him. All armed with similar swords, circling, looking for an advantage. Looking for the correct moment to strike.

Before any vampire was accepted into the ranks of Cromwell's Enforcers, they were made to stand a trial of combat. It was no mere formality. The Aspirant had to show skill, courage, and the desire to win.

Obviously, there was no way a single combatant could stand against four experienced Enforcers but that was not the point. The point of the exercise was to see how long they lasted.

And, if Cromwell was impressed enough, the Aspirant was allowed to join their ranks.

One of the Enforcers lunged forward but Nathan slipped out of the way without any apparent effort. As he did so, another struck from behind. Again,

Nathan moved but the edge of the blade slid along his ribs, cutting deeply. Exposing bone.

Cromwell smiled, pleased to see the sneering Aspirant brought down a peg or two. However, his smile did not last long when he saw the deep cut heal up almost instantly. In less than a second.

Cromwell turned to Byron.

'My lord,' he whispered. 'How is that possible? A wound that deep should take minutes to heal. Not microseconds.'

Lord Byron raised an eyebrow. 'I do not know, Enforcer. All I do know is that we have something unique. The blend of Shadowhunter and *Nosferatu* has created a new breed. Now watch.'

Again, the vampires attacked but this time Nathan struck back. Spinning, cutting, and parrying, combining his new speed and strength with his hundred years of Shadowhunter training. He was unstoppable. His blade struck and cut again and again. Whenever an enforcer was badly cut they would simply drop to one knee and stay still. After all, it was not a fight to the death. It was a simple test.

Within seconds the four Enforcers were kneeling, and Nathan stood still. His only wound already totally healed.

Lord Byron clapped. 'Well done, young Aspirant,' he said. 'Now, please go to your rooms and await Master Cromwell's decision.

Nathan nodded, bowed respectfully, and left the room without a glance at the defeated Enforcers.

'Beyond impressive,' commented Cromwell. 'But I still wonder if he can be trusted'

Lord Byron laughed. 'He is *Nosferatu*. His blood is our blood. Of course he can be trusted. That is like asking if we can trust ourselves.'

'Normally I would agree, sire,' said Cromwell. 'But you yourself said that we are dealing with a new species here. Who knows how and what he thinks.'

'He betrayed his Shadowhunter companions. He helped to destroy the Olympus Foundation,' reminded Byron. 'He is desperate to be accepted. Also, he is ambitious. Very ambitious. I would watch him if I were you,

Cromwell,' advised Lord Byron with a grin.

'And I you, my lord,' added the Enforcer. 'However, sire, we have not totally destroyed the foundation. When we took Nathan to see the manor house, he said that one of the Hunters was not present. A Jamaican by the name of Bastian Miller. Also, we could find no trace of the wizard.'

'They are of no moment,' said Byron. 'What worries me is the girl. This Emily Hawk. The crew that we sent to exterminate her did not return. I have placed watchers over Sir William's abode and there is no sign of her. Or him. I feel that, once again, we have underestimated her power.'

'It seems impossible,' mused Cromwell. 'We sent ten brethren after her. She must be beyond superhuman. Unless Sir William helped in some way.'

Lord Byron laughed. 'What? That effete antiques dealer? I think not. Must have been quite a shock for him though. No, we need to hunt this Emily down and destroy her. Our time has come. This is the time of the *Nosferatu* and I won't have some snot-nose little girl-child ruining things.'

'We have all of our Familiars looking out for her, sire,' affirmed Cromwell. 'We shall find her; it is only a matter of time.'

Chapter 25

The apartment was situated in the docks of London. A large warehouse conversion that took up the top two floors of the building. Three-hundred-and-sixty-degree views and wraparound balconies allowed one to observe London and surrounds in its entirety.

There were three bedrooms, all en suite, three reception rooms and an indoor-outdoor gymnasium on the roof terrace.

Emily's days were much of a muchness. She rose early, ate, then trained for three hours. After that, she ate again, showered, and went out if she needed anything.

Then returned and trained again, until exhaustion set in.

There were times when she longed to contact Bart and Ryoko, but she knew that to do so would surely sign their death warrant. She couldn't take the smallest chance of attracting attention to them. The *Nosferatu* would hone in on them and destroy them merely because they meant something to her.

She had phoned William a couple of times, but the conversations were stilted and wary as his concern for her overwhelmed all else and, after the second call, Emily had decided not to contact him again until she was either in trouble, or she had some sort of plan. When she first arrived, she had gone out and purchased some nondescript clothing. Cheap jeans, T-shirts, sneakers, and a baseball cap. She knew that parading about in her black Shadowhunter gear could attract unwanted attention, so instead she donned the attire of a student. With her long blonde hair tucked under the cap, no makeup, and small round sunglasses she blended in with any of the other thousands of comparable types walking the street of the capital city. Anonymous in their similarities.

When she shopped for food she used cash and purchased from the local market as opposed to the chain stores. She never shopped in the same place more than once a week, and never purchased anything unusual. Polite, quiet, and forgettable.

She was alone. But she had no time to be lonely. Her need to improve herself drove her beyond loneliness.

Over the last few weeks she had spent hour upon hour in the apartment's gym, practicing with her sword, beating the heavy punchbag, kicking and striking the *makiwara* Japanese punching board, and performing endless katas that had honed her skills to a level she had never thought possible. She was fitter, stronger, faster, and deadlier than she had ever been.

Because she was determined that the next time she came across a blood sucker, there would only be one possible outcome. They had killed her friends. They had irrevocably changed her life. And they would pay.

It was time for Emily Hawk to kick some serious ass.

It had been a month to the day when she finally donned her Shadowhunter uniform and left the building heading for the city. There she visited a shabby lawyer's office in Brixton, handed them a wad of cash and instructed them to place a series of classified adverts in all of the London and national newspapers. There was no way that she could have done so herself without a credit card and the consequent questions and flags that its use would have raised.

The ad was short and simple, but she knew only one person would fully understand what she was saying.

Bastian. Tings a gwaan but we hab di ting lack. Link me a Ben Johnson day where we got de bashy red dress.

Loosely translated from the Jamaican patois the message read; "Bastian. Things have gone bad, but we need to sort them out. Meet me on Thursday at the shop where I purchased the red dress."

It was the best she could do. Now she simply had to wait two days and then stake out the clothes shop that she and Bastian had visited before.

She had no idea how to track down Nathan.

Chapter 26

The ancient crone absentmindedly stroked the large crow that sat on the back of the kitchen chair while she looked at the body of the man on the floor.

'Ah, Ambros,' she croaked. 'What have you done this time?'

The body had appeared in the old crone's cottage some few weeks back. Materializing out of thin air to land on the floor in her living area. She had recognized him straightaway, even though it had been over a hundred years since she had last seen him. She had also instantly perceived that he was dying. In fact, so close to death was he, she could literally smell the stench of the River Styx on his clothes.

A closer look at his various wounds and her worst fears were realized. *Droch-fhola.* The evil blood. Vampires.

Given time a mage as powerful as the man who lay before her could survive. But he needed time. And that he did not have. So, the old crone had cast a spell. It was done in desperation, but it was all she could think of.

The spell of *Gheimhridh*. The winter spell.

And now the body of Ambros lay still, under a two-inch coating of ice. His heart in stasis. Not alive but not yet dead.

She had given him time. But it had cost her dearly, for although the spell of *Gheimhridh* allowed one to live on borrowed time, it demanded payment in kind.

So, she had sacrificed years of her own life. And even to one who has lived for so long as to be almost immortal, time is a precious resource and not one to be given away lightly. But she would have gladly sacrificed her every last second for the not dead yet not alive man in front of her. For, although she was now known to all as the Morrigan, or the goddess of battle, she remembered well the days when she had been called

Morgan le Fay. Then she had been the oft time lover of the man in front of her. Myrddin Ambrosius Ambros Caledonensis, or Merlin the Magician as most knew him.

Since then, the legend of King Arthur and his mage had been twisted and turned into a mere fable of Camelot and the eventual search for the Holy Grail. But the Morrigan remembered the truth. She remembered the battles and the sacrifices Arthur's knights had made as they fought against the *Nosferatu*. The children of the night.

The terror of the villagers as they became mere fodder for the vampires and how, with the help of Merlin and the Olympus Foundation, they had eventually driven the *Nosferatu* underground so that, once more, the people of Camelot could live in happiness and light.

Since those far flung times, myth and fable had turned the Olympus Foundation into the Knights of the Round Table and Merlin had become known as a mere magician.

But the Morrigan knew – and so she

sacrificed her own time for that of Merlin's.

Because his sageness and wisdom would be needed once again when the dark ones came to the fore.

Chapter 27

Emily had arrived early, perhaps ten minutes before the boutique opened, and she had sat in the window seat of the coffee shop across the street. She nursed two coffees for just over an hour and then left and took a similar seat in a vegetarian snack bar adjacent to the shop she was scoping out.

A yoghurt and a carrot juice later she noticed a short, sturdy Jamaican man walk past the boutique, his dreads ensconced in an oversized black beanie with a Rasta stripe. This was the second time she had seen him, so she decided to get up and follow. Leaving a handful of change on the table, she walked out.

The Rasta man walked slowly but steadily, never looking back or to the side, his eyes straight ahead and his pace measured. After ten minutes he took a left turn. Then another, before he stopped in front of a matt black door recessed into the front of what looked to be a nightclub. The windows were painted black and the exterior, a dark shade of midnight blue.

There was no neon signage or overt advertisements but, using her enhanced eyesight, Emily could make out a discreet brass plaque next to the door.

Club Haile Selassie – Members Only.

The man pushed a button next to the door and waited. It swung open to reveal a dark corridor and, before he went inside, the Rasta turned to Emily, and motioned to her.

She hesitated slightly and then ran across the street and allowed herself to be ushered through the door which was closed behind her.

'How you know about Ben Johnson day?' asked a voice in the darkness.

Emily smiled. 'I remember things,' she replied. 'You know that.' She threw her arms around the lithe Jamaican Shadowhunter who was standing in the gloom. 'You're alive,' she said.

'You too,' laughed Bastian as he stood back from her. 'You looking good, girl.' He punched her upper arm. 'Man, rock solid. You been hitting the gym?'

Em nodded, her expression serious. 'I'm not the little girl you knew a month ago.'

Bastian's face darkened. 'Yeah,' he said. 'Some bad stuff be going down.'

He turned and walked down the corridor, beckoning for Em to follow. They walked into a large wood-paneled room, a fireplace on the one wall, and large windows that looked out onto an enclosed courtyard. Em noticed with amusement that the courtyard had multiple pots growing marijuana plants in them.

There was a long table in the centre of the room and on it was an impressive array of firearms. Semiauto pistols, massive revolvers, mac-10 submachine guns and even an AK47 assault rifle. Piles of ammunition lay scattered casually across the surface and Em could see, by the way the light reflected off the bullets, that the ammo was all silver-tipped.

There were six men sitting in the room and all but one stood up when Emily entered.

'These are my peeps,' said Bastian. He introduced them to Em, pointing to each as he called out their names. 'Tagereg, Stakkie, Qwenga, Banton and Samfy.' He pointed at the man who remained seated. 'That be Don Dada, the big boss of the place. He don't stand so good on account of been crippled.'

Don Dada looked the spit of BB King and he laughed out loud.

'Now, Bastian, boy, I told you I don't be liking that word, "cripple". I be challenged in the working limbs department, that's all. So, don't be introducing me as no cripple, boy.'

'Ah, feel no way, Dada,' replied Bastian. 'I say what I say with love and respect.'

Emily smiled. 'Pleased to meet you mister Dada.'

Don Dada grinned back, showing a row of perfect white teeth and a sizable quantity of gold caps. 'Me no mister to you, lil-girl,' he said. 'You just call me Dada and we gets along fine.'

Em nodded. 'Unusual names you all got,' she noted. 'I'm Emily. Bastian calls me Em, so I suppose that you all will as well.'

The man who went by the moniker of Stakkie nodded. 'Those ain't be our real names,' he explained. 'They be our street names.'

'Yeah,' confirmed Bastian. 'Stakkie is slang for Mental Case. Tagereg means Criminal. Qwenga is Gangster. Banton is Storyteller, and Samfy, Con Man.'

Apart from Bastian and Stakkie who had shown them in, the other four men were all six foot five or six. Tall, well-muscled, and rangy with a palpable well of aggression and arrogance that Emily found both dangerous and attractive.

She could tell straightaway that these were men that were quick to smile and easy to anger. A heady combination and one that would keep anyone on their toes.

'Anyways,' said Bastian. 'Sit. We've called out for pizza and soda. Now we need to catch up.'

They all sat down but before Em spoke she cast a guarded look at Bastian. He nodded to her. 'The boys know all,' he said. 'They may be Yardies that treat the law a little looser than most, but they hate the blood suckers for real. You ask any island boy and he'll tell you he ain't got no truck with monsters or zombies or voodoo.'

'That be correct,' confirmed Dada. 'We sees that crap and we take it out,' he patted the AK47 assault rifle on the table. 'We got the tools and we got the skills. Those vamps must learn that the nighttime streets belong to the Yardies, not the leeches.'

There was a chorus of rumbling agreement from the collected men.

So Em told them her story.

After she had finished, Bastian let out a slow, low whistle. 'Man, you have had a freaky few weeks,' he said. 'Bloodborn, shape-shifters. Going on the run and hiding. I see you're wearing your Shadowhunter outfit now.'

Em nodded. 'That's because I'm not hiding anymore. I'm hunting.'

The Yardies shouted their approval. 'Cool,' said Bastian. 'So, what's the plan?'

Em shrugged. 'Haven't got one. I

thought I'd leave that bit up to you, seeing as you're about a million years old and I'm barely a teenager.'

'Steady,' said Bastian.

Tagereg laughed. 'Dat be true,' he said. 'Grandpa Bastian be make us all like little pickney boys he be so old.'

Bastian shook his head. 'Hey Tagereg, go easy on the patois, right? I mean you went to Oxford University and got a first in English.'

Tagereg shrugged. 'So? I speak how I speak.'

'Well speak normal,' said Bastian. 'At least until Emily learns the lingo. But we need to make a plan. One thing, the vamps must be hurting big time right now. The Shadowhunters and your boys, Sir William and Sylvian, have iced over seventy of them, so I can guarantee you'll all be top of the most hated list right now.'

Em shook her head. 'Not William or Sylvian,' she stated. 'The vamps have no idea that William's a shifter and as far as they're concerned, Sylvian doesn't even exist.'

'Whoa,' interjected Tagereg. 'So, what

you're saying is the vamps reckon that you are pretty much wholly responsible for taking out a huge percentage of their standing force. Man,' he continued. 'I wouldn't give long odds on your survival. They're gonna come after you with everything they got, girl.'

'Shut it, Tag,' warned Bastian. 'I won't have any of that negative talk here, okay?'

'You want me to shut it, why don't you make me,' growled Tag as he stood up, topping out at almost a foot taller than Bastian.

The Shadowhunter raised an eyebrow. 'Really? You want to go there again? Ain't you sick of me beating your ass to a pulp every time you try this crap?'

Tag shrugged. 'Maybe this time I get lucky. Whatever, I'm not accustomed to backing down, so face up, man. Let's go round and round and see what happens.'

Emily stood up, walked over to Tag and, without warning, she punched him in the chest. The big man took off like he'd been hit by a monster truck, flying across the room, and smashing into the wall so hard that chunks of plaster chipped off. Then he slid down the wall and collapsed onto the floor in an untidy heap, his limbs twitching as he lapsed into unconsciousness.

'Look here,' said Emily. 'We don't have time for any of this macho bullshit. Out there are hundreds of blood suckers. They killed our friends. They're looking for us and they aren't going to stop there. If they find the *corona potestatem* who knows what they'll do next. This isn't just about us. It's about the whole of humanity.'

The Yardies stared at the young Shadowhunter and finally Dada spoke. 'Hey,' he said. 'That child jus whipped Tag's ass big time. I reckon dat we make a plan before she get physical wid the rest of us.'

Bastian grinned. 'You speak the truth, Don Dada. Best we get our thinking caps on or Em is gonna tear our arms off and beat us to death with the sticky ends.'

Em stuck her tongue out at Bastian and then sat down. 'Okay,' she said. 'Let's make a plan. I reckon we should get hold of William and Sylvian. See how they can help.'

There was an uncomfortable silence until Don Dada spoke. 'We don't want hang with no monsters,' he said. 'Damn vampire and werewolf.'

'He's a bloodborn,' countered Em. 'And William is a shape-shifter.'

'Sure,' said Dada. 'But if it looks like a tiger and acts like a tiger then I learned long ago that you better not pull its tail, or the damn thing will chew your head off. Listen, girly, I don't mind my people helps to hunt down the dark ones but don't ask me to team up wid de monsters. We Yardies fight the good fight but we does it alone.'

There was a groan from the corner and Tag pulled himself slowly to his feet. He shook his head and looked around the room. 'Man,' he grunted. 'I just been smashed by a little girl-sized truck. Damn, babe, where'd you learn to punch like that?'

'I'm not your babe, Tagereg,' snapped Emily. 'Now are you going to behave?'

'If I don't are you gonna beat up on me

some more?'

Em nodded. 'For sure.'

Okay,' answered Tag. 'Then I'll behave. But I'm still going to have to agree with the boss man.

We don't work with no monsters. Period.'

'Well then have you got any better suggestions?' asked Em.

'Sure. It's simple. We get our street merchants to keep an eye out for vamp-whores. Then we follow them to the suck-fest and kill their masters.'

'Not sure I understood that completely,' admitted Em.

'It's a good idea,' interjected Bastian. 'What Tag is saying is that we get our merchants, the dudes that sell our ganja on the streets, to keep an eye out for familiars. Young guys and girls that are looking to hang out with the vamps. As soon as we get a line on them, we follow them back to their master's hang out and when the vamps are feeding we attack and kill them.'

'You can do that?' asked Em.

'Sure,' affirmed Tag. 'We got hundreds of salesmen. And there be many Goths and Vamp-lovers out there. We just keep a track on all of them and pretty soon one of them will lead us to a nest. Bish, bash, bosh – we go and machine gun the leeches to death. Then we just keep doing that. Wash, rinse, repeat.'

'I like it,' said Em. 'It's simple.'

'Yeah,' laughed Bastian. 'Like Tagereg.'

Tag didn't laugh. 'Yeah, Bastian,' he said. 'You just been all cheeky 'cause you know that the little girl will tear Tag a new asshole if he beats on you.'

Bastian laughed louder, and Tag had the decency to join in.

Chapter
28

Kevin no longer went by his given name. Ever since he and three friends had started the *real vampire website.com* they had taken on more suitable monikers. He had decided on Tarquin. Simon had become Constantine. Brian changed his name to Cyprian and Debbie, the only girl in the group, was now known as Cordelia.

They had written up a list of thirteen rules that applied to anyone who wanted to be a member of their house and, although no one had yet applied, Kevin/Tarquin insisted all of the rules would be stringently adhered to.

Cyprian had complained, saying that most of the rules were either lame or were simply a differently worded repetition of the first three rules. But Tarquin had explained that any list to do with the arcane had to have thirteen points. I mean, like, it's not as though vampires work on the decimal system, you know. He had told them. No self-respecting *Nosferatu* would ever make a list of ten points. Or even twelve, I mean, really, what are they? Like bakers or something?

And anyway, most of the points were to do with how to dress. All of the members were in agreement that the most important thing about being a vampire fledgling, is the uber-cool dress sense. Firstly, black, black, and more black. Secondly, piercings were cool, tattoos were cooler, and it was imperative to wear loads of chunky jewelry featuring inverted crucifixes, the number 666 and Victorian looking amulets.

The four of them frequented a number of the better-known Goth clubs and vampire hangouts in London. Places like "The Blood and Velvet" in Holloway Road or the "Being Boiled" in Notting Hill Gate.

But this was the first time they had visited a lesser known club, situated off a cramped side street in Kings Cross.

The club was known as "The Clinic", and the moment Tarquin and his friends had entered they knew it was the real deal.

They had been checked in at the door, as entrance was by invitation only. Tarquin had garnered an invite the weekend before when a cool looking dude, dressed all in black with the palest skin imaginable, had approached him at the "Blood and Velvet" and asked if he would like to try a new club. He had assured Tarquin that this was the proper business. No role playing or pretending. Real vampires, real blood. Proper *Nosferatu*. And he had flattered Tarquin enormously, calling all the other Goths, Wanabees, Pretenders and Posers. Tarquin had accepted with alacrity and the dude had told him he was welcome to bring some friends, as long as they were of a similar caliber.

And so here they were. All four of them had been seriously nervous before coming, knowing that this could be their break into the big time. The real McCoy, as it were. So, Cyprian had contacted their usual dealer and purchased a couple of ounces of weed off him. He had told the Rasta about the club, boasting they were now part of an elite, as opposed to the children that were merely playing at being familiars. And the Jamaican dealer had seemed impressed, asking many questions, and then wishing Cyprian good luck.

They had smoked themselves into a more mellow state of mind and then left for the club, arriving relaxed and comfortable.

The place was large and well-appointed. A bar ran the length of the one wall and a selection of low tables and wingback chairs were scattered about the room. Along the other wall, a row of curtained private booths stood in semi-darkness.

The music was a combination of jazz fusion and funk. No throbbing house beats or sticky modern pop. And the volume was low enough to enable one to have a decent conversation without shouting raucously into their ear.

The group of teenagers went to the bar

and ordered vodka, straight up. They would have preferred something sweeter, an alcopop or a 'something-and-coke' but vodka was cool. And being cool was what it was all about.

No sooner had they received their drinks than a stunning young man came walking over to greet them.

'Hi,' he said with a smile, his fangs glinting slightly in the low light. 'It's good to see newcomers at the club. My name is Patrick.'

Tarquin introduced himself and the rest of the group. Patrick raised an eyebrow. 'Tarquin? Cordelia? Oh, how deliciously Victorian' he said. 'Tell me, is this your first time at a real *Nosferatu* club?'

They all nodded, while at the same time trying to look cool and self-assured.

'And have you ever communed with one of us before?'

They shook their heads.

'But we are keen to serve,' assured Cordelia, desperate to garner the vampire's approbation.

'Ah, virgins,' breathed Patrick with another fang-revealing smile. 'Well don't be nervous,' he assured. 'Tell you what, why don't you join me and a couple of my friends in one of the private booths. We can talk and...' he paused for a second. 'Drink.'

The four friends followed Patrick to one of the curtained booths that lined the wall. He pulled the curtain aside to reveal a surprisingly large area. A central table and two long couches. More than ample room for the four friends, plus Patrick and the two more vampires already sitting there.

The other vamps looked like a couple, a man similar in appearance to Patrick and a blonde woman with short-cropped hair and a face straight out of Vogue magazine.

Patrick introduced the four newcomers and the female vampire chuckled, low and throaty. 'Gosh,' she said. 'Surely those aren't your real names? Good god, where did you find them? Old Addams family movies?' She stood up and held out her hand. 'My name is Morticia and this here is Gomez.' All three vamps laughed. 'Not really,' the blonde continued. 'I'm Sally. This gentleman here is Toby.'

Tarquin took Sally's hand and, as he did, she pulled him towards her, lifting his feet off the ground with her strength.

He slammed up against Sally's body with an audible thump that took his breath away.

She sniffed his neck. 'Mmm. Yummy,' she purred as her fangs slid out over her bottom lip.

'They're virgins,' informed Patrick as he motioned the other three friends to sit down on the sofas. Tarquin stayed standing, held upright by Sally's iron grip.

'So, you kids want to get into the vampire scene?' asked Toby.

They nodded collectively, like a crew of bobble heads on a car dashboard.

'Why?' enquired Patrick.

'Well it's just so, like uber-cool,' answered Cordelia. 'You all look so good and then there's that everlasting life thing.'

'And the sick clothes,' added Cyprian.

'I see,' noted Toby. 'So, tell me before we become really good friends. What are your real names?'

Cyprian looked embarrassed, but Toby assured him. 'Don't worry,' he said. 'A name is nothing and we wouldn't want to start our relationship off with a lie, would we?'

'I'm Brian,' admitted the ex-Cyprian. 'That's Simon, Debbie, and Tarquin is actually Kevin.'

'See now, that wasn't so difficult, was it?'

Brian smiled and nodded. 'So now we're friends?' he asked hesitantly.

Patrick laughed in genuine amusement. 'Oh please,' he said as he leaned forward and grasped Brian by the throat.

'You're nothing more than meat. And why would we possibly want to fraternize with the food?'

Brian thrashed about, but Patrick's grip was stronger than steel. At the same time Sally bared her fangs and savagely bit into Kevin's neck, throwing her head from side to side as she tore deeply into his jugular. Blood poured out, running over her lips and down her chest.

Debbie started to scream but it died in her throat as Toby jumped across the table and bit into her.

Simon turned to run but as he did, Toby grabbed his arm and bit his wrist. In desperation Simon pulled away and ripped the curtain aside. And then a massive explosion rocked the room. He saw a group of men running in through the broken door that had been blown off its hinges. They were all wielding automatic weapons.

Leading them was a tall blonde angel with a Japanese sword.

The room erupted in pandemonium as vampires attacked the interlopers, familiars ran screaming for cover, and the angel strode forward, swinging her sword like the very vision of the goddess of death herself. All about her, blood suckers were flung aside as she causally decapitated them, her sword weaving a gossamer pattern of light in the fetid atmosphere.

One of the men turned towards Simon who dropped to the floor as the man opened up with his automatic weapon. Slugs buffeted the air above the teenager and he could hear them slamming into the vampires behind him.

And then she was there, stepping over him, her sword a flash of red and silver. He felt the warm vampire blood spray over his back as she dealt her cards of death once more.

Simon peered up to see another man with a sword. He was moving around the room, decapitating any vampire who was on the floor. The angel stepped back over him and looked down.

She held out her hand. 'Get up.'

Simon took it and stood, his legs shaking with the aftermath of his absolute terror.

'I'm sorry,' she said. 'Your friends are dead.' Simon turned to see that she had decapitated Kevin, Debbie, and Brian. Without warning he felt the bile rise in his throat and he bent over double as he threw up.

Tag walked over. 'Yo, Em, why's the boy chucking up?' he asked.

She gestured towards the pile of mutilated bodies. 'His friends.'

He shook his head. 'Well, when you ride the tiger you don't ever get off, cause that's when he eats you. Serves them right for fraternizing with the monsters.'

'Come on Tagereg,' said Emily. 'He's young and stupid. Give him a break.'

Tag nodded. 'Okay. Hey, boy,' he said to Simon. 'You all right?'

Simon nodded and wiped his mouth with the back of his hand.

Tagereg jumped back. 'Oh crap, man,' he exclaimed. 'The boy's been bit.' He pointed at Simon's wrist, the teeth marks blatantly apparent. 'He's gonna have to go, Em. And quick, before he turns.'

Simon turned to the blonde angel for support. 'Please,' he whispered. 'It's just a small bite. I'm sure that it'll be fine.'

'I'm sorry,' she said. And Simon could see that she genuinely was.

The last thing he saw was the silver arc of the sword descending on his neck.

Chapter 29

Bastian had moved into the apartment with Em. At the same time, so had Tagereg who had taken to following Emily around like a six foot six, three-hundred-pound puppy. He had appointed himself as her bodyguard and he took his new vocation deadly seriously, insisting everyone treated Em with respect...or else.

It was the morning after their first hit on the vampire club and Emily was still hugely upset over killing the boy, Simon. She didn't say anything but both Bastian and Tag could tell the extermination had cost her dearly.

Bastian sat down at the kitchen table opposite Em, shook a cigarette out of his pack, lit and inhaled. 'It was a mercy killing,' he said softly. 'He would have died anyway. Or turned. Or worse, he could have become a Grinder. A mindless animal, living forever under the yoke of the blood suckers.'

'He was just a kid,' whispered Em. 'Looking to fit in. Playing games. Damn, he didn't deserve to die.' Tag brought over a mug of tea and handed it to her. She smiled. 'Thanks Tag. You're a good man.'

Tag shook his head. 'No. If I'd killed that kid it wouldn't have bothered me none. Things like that upset good folk. Me, it's just a task, nothing more. You want more sugar in that?'

Em shook her head and forced some of the over-sweetened tea down. For some reason Tag thought that the more sugar he put into a cup of tea, the nicer it was. Initially Em had told him she liked her tea without milk and just a dash of honey, but he had laughed out loud, convinced that she was teasing him.

'Yeah,' he had said. 'Imagine drinking something like that. You don't worry, girly,' he had continued. 'Tag makes a decent cup of tea.'

And he had proceeded to bring her a mug of milky, tea-flavored syrup.

And Emily simply didn't have the heart

to correct him. So now she drank milky, sweet tea.

'Look, Em,' said Bastian. 'It's bad killing an innocent. But the moment you fraternize with the blood suckers, you lose your innocence. It's going to happen again, and you have to harden your soul. Put it behind you. These are the tough decisions that we're going to have to make. Over and over again.'

'Yeah,' added Tag. 'If they don't wanna be dead then they better not play with the monsters.'

'I'll be fine,' promised Em. 'Especially after a mug of Tag's excellent tea.'

Tag beamed so widely it looked as though he was going to swallow both of his ears.

'We need to discuss our modus operandi,' said Bastian. 'Last night worked but it was messy and noisy. I had to pull in a lot of favors and spend a lot of money to cover things up. Luckily, I've still got access to the Foundation's funds, so money is no object, but we simply cannot carry on just machine gunning Vampire nests. Sooner or later the coppers are going to come down hard and we don't want that.'

'But that's always been our way,' argued Tag. 'We hit our enemies hard and fast and messy. Send out a message. Don't mess with the boys from back-of-the-yard.'

'Well that's going to stop,' said Bastian. 'This isn't some petty gang war. It's about the continuation of the human species. So, from now on we go in quieter. I'll organize some silencers for the MAC-10 sub machine guns and also for the Glock pistols. We're going to have to lose the AK's and the shotguns. Stealth is going to be our watchword from now on.'

'I still think we should involve William and Sylvian,' suggested Em. 'And we need to find Nathan.'

Bastian shook his head. 'Not gonna happen. Firstly, if Nathan is hiding, we will never find him until he wants to be found. And, secondly, regarding your mates, maybe if it was just me it would be a go, but the Yardies don't work with monsters.'

'They're not monsters,' argued Emily.

'William's real nice and Sylvian has saved my life twice.'

'To us they all monsters,' said Tagereg. 'Vamps, werewolves, zombies, shape-shifters. They're things you scare children with to make them behave. Monsters. Don't matter if they good or if they bad, they all non-human so they be monsters to us.'

'What about Bastian and me?' asked Em. 'Shadowhunters. Aren't we non-human monsters?'

Tag laughed. 'No ways, girly,' he said. 'You dudes is enhanced humans. You all good with us.'

***

Three days later Em and her Yardies hit a vampire lounge in a basement in Islington.

And this time it was a very different operation. They came in through the back entrance. No explosions. Samfy had picked the lock after disabling the single security camera with a slingshot.

The back room was a small store full of liquor and that led to a kitchen. The kitchen, however, was empty. Unused.

The Yardies slipped through, Tag on point with Emily right behind him. Then they burst into the club, weapons hot.

It was a single large room. Dim lights as per usual. Curved sofas and low tables were scattered randomly about the room and small groups of vamps were feeding, three or four to each human. Unlike the other times that Em had seen them take suck, these vamps were actually being quite tender. Nibbling and licking at their victim's blood as opposed to tearing and rending their flesh.

For some reason Em found it worse than the usual bloody mayhem that the blood suckers called feeding. It was more intimate. Sexual.

The vamps were taken by complete surprise. Silenced weapons spat silver death. Em and Bastian whirled like steel-bladed dervishes, cutting through the blood suckers and their bitten-victims.

Not one being survived. All vamps were dispatched. And every victim, as they had all been infected.

Emily's blade ran red with the blood of both monster and human alike.

They left via the same way they had entered. Stealthy. Silent. But for the almost imperceptible sound of Emily's quiet weeping.

As they had after the last hit, the group split up. The Yardies heading back to their hangout and Em, Bastian and Tag heading for the apartment.

The three friends arrived back on foot. Tag entered first, flicking on the main lights when he did. As the lights went on someone, or something, grabbed the six foot six, three-hundred-pound Yardie and threw him across the room like he was a puppet. He hammered into the kitchen table and rolled off, breaking two chairs as he smashed into them on his way down.

He made to stand up, but another man stood above him, a drawn rapier held at his throat. 'I think not, *mon ami*,' he said. 'Unless you want me to spill your lifeblood out onto the floor.'

Sylvian smiled and slid his sword back into his scabbard.

Bastian readied himself to fight but before he could attack, Emily shouted out.

'Stop. They're friends.' She turned to face William. 'What the hell do you think you're doing, throwing Tag around like that?'

William didn't back down as he usually did. 'How was I to know he was on your side? How was I to know that these two hadn't forced you to bring them back here? In fact, Emily, how was I supposed to know anything as you haven't bloody phoned me for weeks now? Sylvian and I thought you were in trouble. And then I hear, via the grapevine, that you've launched an all-out war on the *Nosferatu*. Without even telling me.'

'You're not my keeper,' yelled Emily. 'And someone has to fight the fight. Because I don't see you doing it.'

'No,' agreed William. 'But it would have been common courtesy to keep me in the loop. I have managed to stay under the wire for a few hundred years and now, thanks to you, every Familiar and informer is watching me, trying to figure out where I fit into this whole scenario. And you know what? It's only a matter of time until someone works out what I am. And let me tell you something for nothing, Miss self-righteous, fight-the-good-fight, bloody Hawk. The only thing vampires hate more than Shadowhunters, are werewolves.'

'You're not a werewolf,' argued Emily.

'That's bloody semantics, Emily. And you know it.' William clenched his fists in front of himself as he tried to control his anger.

Tagereg, thinking that William was about to strike Emily, leapt up and ran towards her. But before the big Jamaican got moving, Sylvian casually back-handed him across his chest, not even bothering to close his fist.

Once again, the massive Yardie flew across the room, smashed into the wall, and crumpled to an unconscious heap on the floor.

Bastian threw up his hands. 'Alright, everyone just calm down. Sir William, you remember me?'

William nodded. 'Chief inspector, I

think it was.'

Bastian shrugged. 'Obviously not. I'm a Shadowhunter. One of the last few left in the United Kingdom at the moment. Anyway, I think we should all take a breath, brew up some tea, and have a civilized chat. Okay?'

Both Sylvian and William nodded.

In the corner of the room, Tag shook his head and mumbled. 'Tea? I can do that. Might as well, it seems that I ain't no bodyguard any more. Even the little Frenchman beat the crap out of me with a single bitch-slap.'

Emily went over and helped the big man to his feet. 'Rubbish, she said. 'It was a sucker punch and you weren't expecting it. I'll make the tea. You relax, get your strength back, you're still my bodyguard and I need you sharp.'

Tag grinned. 'Yeah, cool. That's right.' He pointed at Sylvian. 'Next time, brother, I be waiting for you. Then we gonna set to. No more sucker-punching Tag.'

Sylvian nodded. 'Next time, mister Yardie man.'

Tag, Bastian, and William sat at the kitchen table and Emily put on the kettle.

But before Emily could brew up the tea, Tag did a spectacular double take as the conversation caught up with him. 'Whoa,' he exclaimed. 'Time out.' He jumped to his feet. 'Just before the little French dude smacked me across the room, did I hear you say that you was a werewolf?' he accused William.

William nodded. 'Technically I'm a shape-shifter, but, yes.'

'Oh no,' continued Tag. 'Then that would make this dude the vampire Em was talking about.'

'Bloodborn,' said Sylvian with a sigh. 'Not vampire.'

'Crap,' yelled Tag. 'I don't hang with no monsters.'

'Stop it, Tag,' commanded Emily. 'That's enough. They're friends of mine and you will be polite to them. They are not werewolves and vampires. In fact, the two of them have probably killed more monsters, as you put it, than every Yardie that ever existed.'

Tag raised an eyebrow. 'That true?' he

asked Sylvian.

The bloodborn nodded. 'Thousands. But then I have been hunting down blood suckers for many hundreds of years now, so I do have a slight advantage over you.'

Tag thought for a few seconds and then nodded. 'I suppose if you be killing monsters then you can't be one yourself.'

Both Sylvian and William nodded.

'Also, being...umm...supernatural or whatever,' continued Tag. 'That would make you mega-strong.'

Again, they nodded.

'Cool,' finished Tag. 'That means, technically, I'm still a badass. It's just that I'm a human badass. Can't really compete with the X-men or whatever.'

Emily put down the mugs of tea on the table and then shoveled another four spoons of sugar into Tag's. 'That's right, Tag,' she confirmed. 'You're still the baddest. Human, that is.'

Tag smiled, sipped his tea, paused, and then added another three spoons of sugar, his fragile ego repaired.

'Look, Emily,' said William. 'I'm

concerned. You've got to stop this gung-ho plan of attack. It's juvenile. Clumsy.'

'I know what I'm doing,' argued Em.

William shook his head. 'No,' he disagreed. 'You don't. You only think you know what you're doing. Sylvian and I have been fighting these abominations for many generations now. You simply cannot underestimate them. They don't think in the same terms that we do. Well, that you do. Short term doesn't exist to them. They are patient beyond belief. They think in years as opposed to days. Centuries. Eons. I beg you, pull back for a while. Stop, think.'

Em shook her head. 'They killed my friends. They are a threat to human existence. Perhaps your age has brought with it an unnecessary caution,' she suggested. 'Maybe your immortality has blinded you to the worth of human life. The preciousness of every hour that a normal mortal has. If I stop and think, people die. Every moment of thoughtful contemplation will result in more human deaths. No,

William,' she insisted. 'Humans are dying so I have to react in a human time frame. Trust me, we are badass. We hit hard and fast, the vamps don't stand a chance.'

William reached across and took Emily's hand. 'Sylvian and I will come with you,' he said. 'Extra protection.'

Em shook her head. 'I'm sorry,' she said. 'The Yardies won't accept you. Don Dada will go mental. It's the whole, monster thing. Anyway, I've got Bastian and Tag. I'll be fine. Trust me.'

Sylvian stood up. 'Well, that's it,' he said. 'Our work is done. Some lessons have to be learned on a personal basis. Because, let's face it, it is hard, if not impossible, to know more than an eighteen-year-old girl.'

Without another word the Frenchman strode from the room and out of the front door. William stood and followed him.

Just before he got out of the front door Emily caught up with him, grabbed his face and kissed him soundly. 'Thank you for caring,' she breathed. 'But this is something I have to do. It's what I am. A Shadowhunter.'

William kissed her back, pressing his lean body up against her. She could feel his heartbeat thumping in his chest. Feel his need for her. His want. His concern. And it took all of her strength to keep herself from grabbing him by the arm and dragging him through to her bedroom to finally have some serious alone-time together.

It was William who pulled away first. He raised an eyebrow and then flashed her a grin. 'Be safe.'

Then he left.

Behind her Emily heard Tag say to Bastian. 'That's enough tea for the girly, I think what she needs now is a bucket of cold water instead.'

And Emily couldn't have put it better herself.

Chapter 30

The club was situated in Camden Town. Past the canal lock, down an almost invisible side street, there was a single-story warehouse. The windows were filthy, and the doors scarred and unpainted. But if one looked closely it became obvious that the dilapidation was a mere facade. A Hollywood set. Post-Apocalyptic chic, the scars by design and the filth applied by hand.

A simple but effective camouflage for a private club situated in the beating heart of an area that boasted a thriving nightlife.

Emily and her Yardies had cased the joint the day before and found a side room that was full of boxes and old furniture. They had decided to enter through this room, via the large set of windows. Samfy had disabled the alarm wires that were linked to the windows and then cut out one of the panes. After that it was a simple process to raise the latch, open the window and climb in.

Once in the room the team did a quick weapons check.

'Right, boys,' said Em. 'Let's go do some harm to the dark ones.'

She opened the door into the warehouse and they filed out into the corridor. At the end of the short corridor was another door. Again, Emily eased it open and peered around. It led directly into the club. A huge single room that had been divided up into smaller areas using shoulder high screens. Almost like a miniature maze. Various types of tables, chairs and sofas were laid out in the maze and a bar ran the whole length of the opposite wall. A multitude of mirror balls reflected snowflakes of light about the room and red spots wove back and forth like pinpoints of fire.

The music was an eastern influenced jazz, using sliding syncopations and based on the Arabic Freygish scale. Like a snake charmer with a drum set. It set Emily's teeth on edge, the notes jarring against her western sensibilities.

Em wasn't tall enough to see directly over the maze of partitions so Tagereg, at six foot six, cast his eyes over the set up.

'Seems almost empty,' he whispered into her ear. 'Maybe ten people scattered around. They all sitting singularly. None in groups. With this weird lighting and the sparkle of the mirror balls, I can't make out if they're vampires or not.'

'This isn't right,' commented Stakkie. 'My informant told me that this place would be buzzing. He reckons it gets well full of blood suckers every Thursday night. Sometimes a hundred or more.'

'I don't like this,' said Emily.

'No worries,' commented Tag. 'I'll just go grab one of these dudes and ask him where all the vampires at.'

'Wait,' said Em. But it was too late. With Tag, thought and deed happened almost simultaneously. He strode into the maze, approached the first person, and pulled him to his feet, studying him closely as he held his MAC-10 submachine gun ready in case he was attacked.

'They're all humans,' he called back over his shoulder. 'And they're either well drunk or drugged.' He shook the man a couple of times and then dropped him. He crumpled to the floor like he was asleep. Tag shrugged and turned to walk back.

But as he did so his face registered shock and, without warning, he opened up with his submachine gun, the silenced rounds tearing out at a rate of eight per second.

A body that seemed to have literally materialized in front of him was picked up by the stream of silver-tipped lead and thrown backwards, shrieking in agony.

'Vamps,' shouted Tag. 'Everywhere. They're lying down, hiding in the shadows below the partitions.'

As he shouted his warning, black clad vampires seemed to boil out of the ground. Ten, twenty, thirty. Countless.

The Yardies opened up, with long raking bursts of fire. Blood spayed into the air as the bullets struck flesh. Bastian and Emily charged forward, their swords weaving a destructive pattern in the air, cutting and slicing.

Em heard a shout of pain and saw Stakkie go down. A vamp latched on to him as he was reloading. Then another, and another. They tore at his flesh, opening his throat and spilling his life out onto the carpet.

With three mighty blows, Emily dispatched them. Stakkie looked up at her with pain-filled eyes.

'Do it,' he croaked from his ruined throat. 'Do it, girly before I turn.'

Emily choked back her tears as she slashed downwards, bringing an end to Stakkie's life.

But there was no time to pause. No time for regret. No time for human feelings.

She jumped forward, parried a dagger wielded by a human familiar and then slashed upwards, disemboweling him with one stroke. He fell to the floor, his intestines rolling out of his wound like so much offal.

Tagereg had picked up Stakkie's machine gun and now wielded one in each hand, firing in short controlled bursts. 'Damn,' he shouted. 'They got us good. Ambushed us. Crap, we should have seen this coming.'

He moved forward, firing, and kicking as he did so. Em watched his back, cutting down any vamps that got close to him.

Out of the corner of her eye she saw Qwenga go down under a pile of blood suckers. And then Samfy. But both of them got back to their feet, firing their weapons, driving back their attackers, genuine smiles plastered across their faces.

'Yeah, you don't get me that easy,' shouted Qwenga. He looked across at Emily. 'No bites,' he called. 'I's clean.' He reloaded his MAC 10 and carried on killing.

'And I,' added Samfy.

But there were simply too many of them. And every vamp took an incredible amount of damage before they were neutralized.

Finally, Emily, Bastian and the remaining Yardies were forced into a circle, no longer attacking. Simply defending.

Fighting for their lives.

'I'm almost out of ammo,' yelled Tag.

'Me too,' shouted Samfy.

There was a chorus of agreement from the other Yardies who were burning through ammunition at a horrendous rate, shiny brass cartridge cases spewing from their weapons and covering the floor like discarded costume jewelry.

Man, thought Emily to herself. It just can't get any worse than this.

And then the ceiling imploded.

Roof tiles buzzed through the air like shrapnel, exploding against the walls or smashing into exposed flesh. Whole sheets of corrugated iron spun across the room like giant blades, severing limbs of human and vampire alike. Large wooden beams crashed to the floor, crushing and maiming.

And then something came leaping down from out of the explosion and landed in the center of the room, legs astride, carrying the biggest machine gun that Emily had ever seen.

A Garwood electrically driven Gatling gun. The type normally mounted on a helicopter. Its barrels revolved as it spat out silver coated lead slugs at a rate of just over 3200 a minute. That is fifty-four bullets a second. It sounded like a giant, tearing telephone books in half with one long continuous growl. The noise was beyond belief.

Vampires simply exploded as the massive quantities of ordnance tore them to shreds.

The Yardies threw themselves to the floor, as did Bastian and Emily.

Em looked up from her prone position to see that it was none other than William, the Wolfman standing in the middle of the room. Incongruously her mind took in the scene and immediately started to work out how much his ordnance actually weighed.

The Gatling gun came in at ninety-five pounds, three thousand rounds of ammunition at a further three hundred pounds and the two car batteries needed to drive the motor, another hundred and twenty. A total of five hundred and fifteen pounds. And he was wielding it like an assault rifle.

The fact that he had transformed into

his Wolfman mode probably had something to do with it, as he stood over eight-foot-tall and his muscles bulged out like sacks of leather filled with nests of fighting snakes as they swelled and rippled.

And then the ammunition was expended, and the only sound was the whirr of the barrels as they spun round. That stopped as well. Silence.

William threw back his head and howled. The sound reverberated about the room, shivering the already fragile foundations, and shaking bits of masonry and wood loose, filling the room with dust and debris.

'Now that,' said Tag. 'Is the most seriously kick-ass thing I have ever seen.'

Chapter 31

William, the Wolfman led Emily and her Yardies out via the back entrance and they followed without question. Tag picked up Stakkie's body, carrying it with as much respect as possible as he brought up the rear.

The back door was locked but William, still in beast mode, simply brushed it aside like it was a paper wall hanging.

In the alley was a large, Ford Transit, or what Emily referred to as a van. Sylvian stood at the rear and around him, lying on the floor, were the remains of at least five decapitated vampires.

'Come on,' he shouted. '*Vite, vite.* Quickly. Get in the back before more come.'

They all piled into the back of the van while Sylvian got behind the wheel. William threw the Gatling gun and accessories in after them and then clambered onto the passenger seat, changing back to his human form as he did so. He grabbed a pair of track pants and a T-shirt out of the glove box and pulled them on before turning to address everyone. 'Is everyone alright?' he asked. 'Have any of you been bitten?'

'We be fine,' answered Tag. 'But Stakkie is well broken. His head isn't here.'

'What do you mean? What happened to it?' asked William.

'I think Emily chopped it off,' answered Tag.

'He asked me to,' objected Emily. 'He didn't want to turn.'

'Hey,' reassured Tag. 'Ain't none of us blame you, sweet-thing. You did the good and brave thing. I was just answering the Wolfman.'

'Dude, we gotta go back for Stakkie's head,' said Samfy.

'Ain't no way, man,' countered Tag. 'We can bury him without his head. It's still him. Well, most of him anyway.'

Emily curled up and leaned against the door, closing her eyes, and fighting back tears. It was her fault. She had pushed too hard and too fast and led her boys straight into an ambush.

If it hadn't been for William, there was no doubt that they would have been killed. Or far worse. Turned. She shuddered. The thought of becoming a vampire filled her with such dread that she almost threw up. Her stomach cramped, and she could feel a trickle of cold sweat run down her back.

And then without warning she burst into floods of tears. Her body shook with emotion and she couldn't catch her breath. She felt as though her lungs were about to burst. Black shadows flickered across her vision and she could hear her heartbeat thumping in her chest.

The vehicle shifted, rocking slightly on its springs and then she felt William sit down next to her. Her put his arms around her and pulled her tight, enveloping her with his arms and chest. Comforting her. Protecting her.

Once again, she was surprised at the massive amount of heat his body generated, and she snuggled as close as she could, letting the warmth cocoon her.

Within seconds exhaustion overcame her and she fell into a deep sleep.

***

Emily woke to find herself being carried like a small child. She didn't need to open her eyes to know she was in William's arms.

Not only could she feel his heat, but she could smell him. That unique, clean leather and ozone musk that enveloped her like a summer's morning in an Alaskan spring. Steel and Pine trees and freshly cut grass.

'You're awake,' he said.

'Mmm,' mumbled Emily. Not yet prepared to face the world in any way whatsoever. Not even to communicate.

'You've been asleep for almost three hours.'

'Where are we?' she asked.

'The New Forest. The Yardies are back with their boss, except for Tag who wouldn't leave you. Don't think he fully trusts Sylvian or me. And, of course, Bastian is with us. I thought we needed to get out of London. Re-plan and re-strategize.'

William pushed a door open as he spoke, and Emily finally opened her eyes. She saw it was still dark outside, then William nudged the door closed. They were in a large, low ceilinged building. Stone walls, exposed beams that were black with age and a rough stone floor.

William placed her back onto her feet. 'This place has been in my family for many generations,' he said. 'It's a hunting lodge. But it's registered as crown property, so no one knows I actually own it. We're safe here from any attacks or prying eyes. The locals are all loyal to me. No one will get close to this place without me knowing about it.'

'Where are the others?' asked Em.

'It's getting dangerously close to sunrise,' answered William. 'So Sylvian is down in the cellar. Bastian is in the kitchen with Tag. They're stoking up the coal stove. Bastian's going to cook, and Tag said he'll make us a pot of tea.'

Emily grimaced at the thought of Tag's tea but said nothing as she followed William through the house and into the kitchen.

Chapter 32

Lord Byron stood still and studied his own feelings with a detachment born of hundreds of years of self-inspection. And he was shocked when he finally worked out what the strange emotion was.

Fear.

Not a fear of any physical harm, although that was a distinct possibility. No, this was a fear of failure. A fear of losing seven hundred years of planning and maneuvering that had brought him to the pinnacle of leadership as the Grand Master of the United Kingdom House of the *Nosferatu*.

But even he had to admit he had not covered himself in glory over the past few weeks.

Failure had been piled on top of failure as he had not managed to completely wipe out the Olympus Foundation, letting the wizard, the girl and another

Shadowhunter escape. He had blundered once again when he had tried, unsuccessfully, to exterminate the girl the second time.

Then he had not foreseen her teaming up with the London Yardies who had proceeded to exact a terrible toll on his brethren, bringing the true death to scores of them as they attacked two of his clubs.

Then when he had finally caught up with them, he had instructed Cromwell to lay a trap and it had all gone horribly wrong. Once again, he had failed to see what had been in front of him the whole time. Sir William was a shape-shifter.

And not just any shape-shifter. No, according to the few vampires that had escaped his wrath at the Camden Club ambush, he was the fabled Omega Wolf, the one wolf who controlled all others. The Alpha of all Alphas. Bigger, faster, and stronger than a normal werewolf. Capable of assuming a man and wolf hybrid mode.

Personally, Lord Byron did not believe them, the myth of the Great Wolf had been bandied about for centuries but he, for one, had never seen him. However, there was no denying that Sir William was most definitely a creature of great power.

Whatever his beliefs, the unthinkable had happened. Janus Augusta, the head of the Italian house and also the *Capo di tutt'i capi* of the Federation had travelled once again from Italy to England in order to personally take over the running of the purge against Emily and the Olympus Foundation. Such were Lord Byron's losses that the *Capo* had actually brought in reinforcements.

One hundred big hitters, all of them Masters, plus another one hundred Grinders. He had also brought one hundred Familiars so they had people who could operate in the day to search for Sir William, the Yardies, and the Hawk girl.

It probably wasn't actually necessary for the *Capo* to bring over such a large number of reinforcements, but he had done so to prove a point. It was a public slap in the face for Lord Byron.

Basically, the *Capo* was saying, '*Not only do I have to sort out your problems, but I have to even bring my own people to do so.*'

Never in his hundreds of years of command had Lord Chelsea Byron been so publicly shamed. So openly belittled.

The only thing now that the *Capo* could do to further his humiliation was to demote him. And although that was almost unprecedented, it had been done before.

That was what was stoking the fires of Lord Byron's fear. The loss of his position. His power. And with it, his existence.

Because, if he was demoted, then he knew the *Capo di tutt'i capi* would insist on the true death. No one wanted an ex-Grand Master moping about the chapter like some sort of whipped cur, begging for scraps, and souring the atmosphere.

Whatever was about to happen, Lord Byron was sure his humiliation was not yet over. His blunders had been huge, as would be his chastisement.

The door opened behind him and the *Capo* and his entourage entered, led by Cromwell the Enforcer.

The first thing Lord Byron noticed was that none of Cromwell's own Enforcers were with him. Of the twenty-six people that entered the room, Cromwell and Nathan were the only brethren belonging to the United Kingdom chapter. The rest were all from the Italian house.

The *Capo* seated himself on one of the leather wingbacks, steepled his fingers together and stared at Byron, his obscenely long fingernails almost tangling together as they curled around each other. Lord Byron approached the leader of all leaders and prostrated himself flat on the floor in front of him. For he knew that now was not the time for false pride. Now was the time to debase himself as much as possible. To humble himself before his lord and master.

No one spoke for fully five minutes. A seeming eternity.

Finally. 'I am disappointed,' rasped the *Capo*. 'I was here only a few weeks ago and you assured me you had everything under control. The girl was as good as dead, you told me. You guaranteed it. Now I return because, instead of killing the girl, you have killed almost fifty of my children. Not counting the slovenly waste of who knows how many Grinders and countless Familiars.'

Lord Byron said nothing. Nor did he move. He simply lay flat on the floor, arms outstretched in front of him, and waited for his fate.

'Stand,' instructed the leader.

Byron rose slowly to his feet but kept his head down.

'I blame myself,' said the *Capo*.

Byron shook his head. 'No, my lord,' he said. 'It is my fault entirely. You are incapable of making a mistake.'

The *Capo* waved one of his ancient claws in front of his face in dismissal. 'Pish and nonsense,' he said. 'I make many mistakes. But tell me now, Byron,' he continued. 'This new creature that you have created,' he pointed at Nathan. 'Talk to me about it.'

'He is an ex-Shadowhunter, my liege. I turned him only a short while ago, but his growth has been exemplary. The combination of his Shadowhunter genes and the *Nosferatu* has gifted him with unusual strength and capabilities.'

The *Capo* beckoned to Nathan. 'Come here, my child,' he commanded.

Nathan walked over and knelt before the ancient vampire leader who leaned forward and took his face in his hands, turning it from side to side as he inspected him. Then the *Capo* pulled Nathan towards himself and slowly and deliberately licked his neck, his purple tongue rasping across his jugular. He pursed his lips, tasting. Rolling the flavor around in his mouth like a wine connoisseur.

The he leaned back into his chair again. Nathan stayed on his knees, his head down.

'Tell me, Lord Byron,' continued the *Capo*. 'Who did you entrust with this latest botched ambush attempt that your house made?'

'As always I assigned the task to Cromwell the Enforcer. But the failure is mine alone.'

'I shall decide who has failed and who has not,' snapped the *Capo*. 'Or, as in this case, who has failed me the most.' He closed his eyes for a while and sat as still as the dead. Lord Byron started to suspect that he had actually fallen asleep or had gone into some sort of deep fugue state. Then he suddenly spoke aloud, his voice a whip-crack of command.

'Child,' he addressed Nathan. 'Kill the Enforcer.'

Nathan reacted instantaneously, jumping to his feet, and attacking Cromwell in one fluid movement. Cromwell, however, also reacted instantly.

The two beings clashed in a welter of kicks and punches, the movements so fast as to be completely indistinguishable to the mortal eye.

Within mere seconds, hundreds of blows had been thrown and both Cromwell and Nathan were bleeding from numerous cuts. Nathan's wounds, however, healed almost as soon as they appeared, whereas Cromwell's took a little longer to knit together.

The *Capo* smiled in pleasure. 'Look,' he said to no one in particular. 'The child's healing process is phenomenal.'

As the fight progressed it became obvious Nathan was by far the superior warrior. Cromwell had grown complacent as the decades had passed, surviving on his reputation more than his actual physical prowess. Whereas Nathan had trained every day as a Shadowhunter. And he had trained specifically to kill vampires, something that even an Enforcer did not specialize in.

In fact, after a few more seconds of hyper-speed combat it became apparent that Nathan was actually toying with the Enforcer. Holding back in order to prolong his humiliation.

The *Capo* cackled with genuine amusement when he realized what the ex-Shadowhunter was doing.

'Enough,' he said as he chuckled. 'Games are over. Finish him, my child.'

And Nathan casually grabbed Cromwell by the throat and tore out his jugular. Then, with a quick twist, he plucked his head off, walked over to the master of masters and presented him with it.

The ancient vampire took the head from the ex-Shadowhunter and held the jagged stump of the neck to his mouth, sucking on it like a gourmand trying to remove the marrow from a soup bone. When he had removed any last traces of blood he threw the detached head to the floor and then reached forward to stroke Nathan's hair.

'Good, my child,' he crooned. 'Lord Byron,' he continued. 'Discipline has been carried out. That is not to say you are blameless but for now, I forgive you.'

Byron sank to his knees once again. 'I thank you, my master.'

'Now, this Nathan. He is your new chief Enforcer. Tell your brethren. When the child speaks, he speaks with my voice. He is now a *Caporegime*.'

Lord Byron nodded and, somehow, managed to keep his look of shock and disbelief off his face. To be considered a *Caporegime* to the master of masters was a privilege that few ever experienced.

Even Lord Byron himself had never been honored in such a way. A *Caporegime* was almost a member of the master's family.

He was to be trusted and obeyed above all others except for the Grand Master of his house.

Ostensibly, it made Nathan Tremblay the second most powerful Nosferatu in the United Kingdom. And he was only days old. A child.

Swallowing his pride, Lord Byron stood and bowed to Nathan. 'Well done, young *Nosferatu*,' he said. 'This is a high honor indeed.'

'Yes,' added the *Capo*. 'Now rise, my child, and sit here by my side for a while.' The old vampire waved the others away. 'Leave me now. I have things to discuss with the child. Go. Go and return only when I call.'

And his ancient red eyes stared at Nathan with a look of lust that he was unable to control.

Chapter 33

The Morrigan ran her fingers along the ice that coated Merlin's arm. He was still in a deep state of hibernation, but she could see he was healing himself. The prodigious well of magic he stored in his very soul was slowly conquering the vampire virus that caused the human physiognomy to change into that of the undead.

But it would be many moons until one would actually be able to class the master magician as truly 'alive'.

However, the goddess of battle was concerned. She could feel in her bones that war was coming. A great war.

Not like many of the ones that she remembered from recent years, more like the wars of old. During the times of King Arthur and his Shadowhunters. A battle of light against dark. And she knew that this battle would be epic. Perhaps beyond the limited recourses of the humans that would be arrayed against it. She needed Merlin to be whole once again. His knowledge and power would be an absolute necessity in the upcoming months and years.

Using her magiks she cast a scrying spell, searching out any and all that had come in contact with Merlin over the few weeks before he had transported himself to her domain. And what she saw shocked her even further.

She saw that the Olympus Foundation had all but been destroyed. From what she could reveal, only a young girl and two men remained of what was once mankind's main defense against the darkness. She also saw Sir William Wolfman and Duc Sylvian Bloodborn. This lifted her spirits slightly as both of these creatures were well known to her and their presence bode well.

Then the Morrigan delved deeper, sending her essence out to follow the vampires that had almost killed the magician. Although she could not pin down where exactly they were, she could see a misty simulacrum of their existence.

There were many of them. She concentrated further. Hundreds of Masters, many hundred more Adepts and literally thousands of Grinders. Never before had she sensed such a gathering of the *Nosferatu*.

Then she allowed her senses to wander, seeking out more knowledge. And, like metal to a lodestone she saw him. And despite his wizened and horrific appearance, Morgan knew him instantly.

Janus Augusta.

He was sitting alone in a chair, his eyes closed. As still as the grave. Then his eyes opened, and he looked up and chuckled.

'Morgan la Fay,' he whispered. 'How long has it been? Five hundred years? More?'

'Janus,' gasped the Morrigan. 'I thought that you died after the Battle of Camllan.'

'Oh no,' he denied. 'It is not that easy to kill me. Quite the contrary. I have prospered and am now the head of the Italian house of the *Nosferatu* and also the *Capo di tutt'i capi* of the

Federation.'

'You were always evil incarnate,' sneered Morgan. 'But the next time that we meet in person I shall make sure that there is no mistake. You will suffer the true death.'

Janus laughed. 'I do not think so. In fact, it will not be long now, and I will finally have the *corona potestatem* in my possession. Quake with fear, little godling, for your time grows close to the end. It is our time now. So, run along, crow. There is nothing for you here.'

Knowing that she would garner no more information, Morgan retreated back to her own body, her heart hammering in her chest from the shock of what she had just heard.

And so, it was with great deliberation that she cast aside all current mores and traditions and decided to approach The Council herself. This was unusual in many ways, mainly because Merlin was the only accepted point of liaison between the gods and humanity and that had been the way for many hundreds of years. Also, as a minor god herself, it would be considered most crass for her to show overt support for humanity. So much so that it might even lead to a shunning or brief ostracization. And that would be brief in immortal terms. Perhaps centuries, if not eons.

But she had no choice.

Once again, the woman known as both the Morrigan and Morgan la Fey, stepped outside where she assumed the form of a large crow and took off, beating her wings hard as she headed for the Castro of Altamira, the enormous underground realm ruled over by the Sidhe, or the fey-folk as they were sometimes known. The gods and goddesses of the humans and the keepers of all things magik.

As she flew, the magic began to ripple along her wings.

Blue pulses of pure power, driving her faster and faster until the air was sundered aside. Then with the sound of thunder, the crow that was the Morrigan shattered the sound barrier.

And then she was there. Flying high in the azure skies above the emerald green rolling lands of the Castro of Altamira.

Below her, various different abodes were scattered about the land. Everything from small mud huts to massive looming edifices of marble and bronze. Each dwelling was fashioned after the god or godling that lived in it.

The Formaorian gods of water lived in rude mud huts, whereas king Finvarra and his queen, Aine, lived in a palace of granite and gold. But the Morrigan knew the exteriors of the dwellings meant naught as they were merely the projection of the general legend that surrounded the dweller. The interiors of the abode had nothing to do with the exterior. Not even their size correlated to the exterior footprint. Every dwelling was palatial when one went inside it. Gods were far too truculent and self-absorbed to live in anything else but total luxury.

The Morrigan, as one of the gods of battle, was unusual in that she had chosen a self-impose exile on earth, surviving on peasant fare and living in a humble hovel. She had decided to eke out her existence in poverty, fading from human memory and avoiding the capriciousness of the gods.

But now Merlin was back, and her ire had been peaked. Once again humanity needed the gods and the Morrigan was damned if she would stand by and let darkness overtake all. She had fought the good fight before and she would again.

She headed straight for the palace of granite and gold, knowing that where the king and queen were, there were oft many other gods, playing games of court, carousing, and generally amusing themselves.

She landed in the main throne room, flaring her wings and changing back into human form as her feet touched the floor. But not the haggard old lady that she was on earth. That simply wouldn't do in the land of the Sidhe, who valued beauty and power above all else. In this land she assumed the form of Morgan la Fay, the siren who was possessed of such beauty that she was able to tempt the celibate magician, Merlin Ambros Caledonensis Aurelius Ambrosius, to her bed chamber. The same Morgan la

Fay who seduced Lancelot, driving him wild with desire for her. The seductress, enchantress, sorceress, and temptress.

And so, she stood in the center of the royal court. Her knee-length lustrous black hair swirling about her naked body like it had a life of its own. Hiding, revealing, and tempting, as it exposed and then covered her naked flesh. The ultimate dance of the veils.

'Morgan!' The king's voice thundered across the room. 'You come uninvited, yet when I call you avoid me.'

Morgan bowed deeply, allowing her hair to part and expose her full breasts, knowing well that they would distract the king. 'My liege,' she said. 'I apologize, I was unavoidably detained.'

'For three hundred years?' he questioned. 'Has it been that long, my king?'

'Yes, it has, Morgan la Fay,' he responded. 'And well you know it.'

'Clothe yourself, battle goddess,' snapped Queen Aine, her jealousy etched into her face.

'I am sorry,' returned Morgan. 'It has

been a while since I was last at court and had no idea we now adhered to the same proletarian morals as the humans.' Morgan clicked her fingers and she was instantly clothed in a silk dress that clung so tightly to her womanly curves it seemed she was now even more naked than before.

'What do you want, Morgan?' asked the king.

'Might I not be here simply to visit?' responded Morgan.

Finvarra shook his head. 'No, you want something Morgan la Fay,' he said. 'You use, you interfere, you take. That is your way. So, out with it.'

Morgan went down on one knee. 'I ask only for a moment of your time, my king.'

'Fine. Talk, I shall give you a moment.'

'The *Dearg Due* are on the rise once more, my liege. And the Shadowhunters are no longer strong enough to resist them. Of late, the Vampires have all but destroyed the Olympus Foundation. Not only that, I have discovered that Janus Augusta is still alive and is now the grand master of the *Nosferatu* Federation.'

The king raised an eyebrow. 'That is disturbing news,' he admitted. 'But I fail to see why you consider it so disastrous.'

'I have communicated with the foul creature,' continued Morgan. 'And he informed me that he is on the very brink of possessing the *corona potestatem.* If he became a Daywalker there will be no containing his power. It will be the end of humanity as we know it. Please, my liege, I beg you. Rally the gods so that we may visit destruction on these foul creatures. Let us once and for all bring an end to them. Scour them from the face of the earth that humanity may live in peace.'

Finvarra threw his head back and laughed out loud. 'Listen to yourself, goddess of battle. So that the humans may live in peace.' He stood up and pointed at Morgan. 'Tell me, Morgan la Fay, when have the humans ever lived in peace?'

'There was a time,' answered Morgan. 'However brief it was, it did exist.'

A shadow of pain flickered over king

Finvarra's face and he cast his eyes down.

'Don't let it be forgotten,' he whispered, almost to himself. 'That once there was a spot, for one brief shining moment, that was known as Camelot.'

'So, you do remember,' said Morgan.

'Of course I remember, Morrigan, goddess of battle,' answered Finvarra. 'I also remember that you were not blameless in the downfall of Camelot. In the death of Arthur. Mankind's last hope for everlasting peace.'

'I was not blameless,' admitted Morgan. 'But neither was I fully to blame. We all gave up. At least I have contrived to live amongst them, to try, in my small way to make up for what I did. But if we let the vampires win then humanity is surely doomed.'

'Humanity dooms itself, Morgan,' stated the king. 'They do not need the dark ones to help them. They destroy their own habitat. Their oceans are choked with the trash of a throwaway society. They war upon each other with weapons that even the most rabid animal would not use. The poor starve at the expense of the rich. With or without the rise of the *Nosferatu*, they are damned.'

'But we can help them,' insisted Morgan.

King Finvarra shook his head sadly. 'No, Morgan la Fay, we cannot. We no longer have the power. Our time has passed. When the humans stopped worshiping us and, instead lay themselves at the feet of the Christian god. Or the Prophet Mohamed. Or even the new gods of technology and greed. Let it go, goddess. Let it go. Now leave, you are not welcome in my home.'

The Morrigan stood tall and looked about the room, trying to catch one of the gods' eyes but they all turned away. 'Not one of you?' she asked. 'You will forsake humanity now, after all these thousands of years?' A single tear slipped down her cheek. 'Not one?'

And so, in the silence of rejection, the Morrigan assumed the guise of the crow once more and transported herself back to the world of the humans.

Chapter 34

'It ain't right,' said Banton. 'I mean, Stakkie was an otherwise SOB but every man deserves to be buried with his head.'

'My boy,' said Don Dada. 'We had no choice. You guys left his head at the club. What else could we do?'

Banton shrugged. 'Nothing. I'm just saying, it ain't right.'

'Rest easy, Banton,' continued Don Dada. 'Come the day of judgment we will all meet on Mount Zion. Praise be to Selassie.'

'Praise him,' agreed Banton.

Don Dada wheeled his chair over to the central table that was, as usual, covered with various firearms and ammunition. 'So, when do you reckon Emily'll get hold of us again?' he asked the room in general.

Qwenga shrugged. 'Not sure Dada,' he admitted. 'That Wolfman that saved our asses done took her away. He seemed mighty pissed at the time, so I reckon that she give us a call when he calms down.'

A loud beep sounded from the corner of the room and all eyes swiveled to the CCTV screens that were installed there. Samfy walked over to take a closer look. 'There's nothing here,' he said. 'Don't know why the alarms went off.' He carried on peering for a while, then picked up the remote control, rewound the DVD and pushed play.

As they all watched they saw a brief blur of movement that lasted for the merest fraction of a second.

'Blood suckers,' shouted Dada.

Everyone ran to the table and grabbed a firearm. As they did so, the window leading from the courtyard exploded inwards and a group of vampires swept into the room. At the same time the front door was ripped off its hinges and the sound of running feet echoed down the entrance corridor as more blood suckers invaded the building.

The deafening chatter of semiauto weapons being fired in an enclosed space echoed about the building as the Yardies opened up with everything that they had.

But resistance was pointless. There were only four Yardies and the vampires kept pouring into the room. This time they had ensured that there would only be one possible outcome.

Qwenga went first, bitten multiple times. Then Banton and finally Samfy. Don Dada sat alone, his wheelchair pulled up next to the table, his pistol empty.

As the gunfire came to an end, Dada pulled a carved wooden box from a satchel attached to his wheelchair and held it to his chest.

A vampire swaggered up to the boss man. 'So, cripple,' he said. 'This is how it ends.'

Dada kept quiet and merely stared back. 'Nothing to say?' continued the vampire. 'Can't walk and can't talk. How sad.'

There was a general ripple of cruel laughter from the other vampires. The room was full of them. Perhaps fifteen in all.

'Everything has to end,' said Dada, eventually. 'We cannot live forever.' He clumsily shifted the box in his grip, trying to hide it next to his body.

'Actually,' contradicted the lead vamp. 'We can. And now it is merely a matter of time before your boys turn and then, perhaps they will also be gifted with immortality. Or perhaps not. Maybe they'll become mere Grinders. Mindless servants. You, on the other hand,' he continued. 'Will have to die. I mean, who wants a crippled vampire?'

Again, the laughter flowed.

'So, what do you have in that box. Old man?' asked the vamp.

'Nothing,' answered Dada. 'It's personal. Please, it's only keepsakes. Mementoes. An old man's memories.'

'Give it to me.'

Don Dada shook his head.

'Don't be ridiculous, old man,' said the vamp. 'Give it to me or I shall tear your arms off and take it anyway.'

Dada looked at the vampire with hatred in his eyes and then he slowly opened the box and fumbled inside. 'Here,' he said as he held out his right hand.

The vampire leaned forward to look. The head Yardie was holding a small handful of wire rings.

'What are those?' asked the vamp. Genuinely interested.

'Nothing of value,' admitted Don Dada. 'Merely the safety pins for the half dozen hand grenades in the box.'

And he smiled.

The resulting explosion ripped through the building like the wrath of God, igniting the gas mains and destroying everything and everyone in a fireball of biblical proportions.

Chapter 35

William switched off the cell phone, stripped the battery out and broke the sim card in half. It was nighttime and the five friends had been staying at his New Forest lodge for a couple of days now as they recovered and attempted to formulate some sort of plan.

'Who was that?' asked Emily.

'One of my retainers,' answered William.

'What did they want?'

William took a deep breath and let it out slowly. Almost as though he were trying to expel his emotions. 'The vamps attacked my manor house last night,' he informed. 'Most of the servants got away. Then the blood suckers fired the place and watched it burn.'

'Oh, William,' gasped Em. 'I'm so sorry.'

The Wolfman shrugged. 'It's just

bricks and mortar. Two of the servants died, that is far more of a tragedy. I have instructed Bartholomew, my chief retainer, to send the servants and their families to my residence on Auskerry Island in the Orkneys. They'll be safe there. It's probably an unnecessary precaution but rather safe than sorry.'

'So, your crib is gone, Wolfman?' asked Tag. 'Yeah,' answered William. 'I'll rebuild it when this is over.'

'But what about all your stuff, man?' continued the Yardie, a look of concern on his face. William smiled. 'No problems, Tag,' he said. 'It's just stuff. Mere possessions. No sweat.'

Sylvian walked into the living room and stood still for a while. 'I am sorry to hear that, Sir William,' he said. 'Although I must admit, over the last hundred years or so, I have almost forgotten what it was like to have a fixed abode. It is difficult in the extreme to live anything approaching a normal life when one cannot venture out during the daytime.'

William nodded.

Then, as if it were a pre-rehearsed

movement, both William and Sylvian cocked their heads to one side, listening to a sound that only they could hear.

The Bloodborn shook his head. 'Impossible,' he stated.

'I agree,' said William. 'Nevertheless, we can both hear her coming.'

And out of nowhere a massive crow appeared in the center of the room, hovering in the air without moving its wings at all. Blue white fire flickered along its body as it contemplated everyone in the room. Cold black eyes like wet pebbles.

'What the hell?' shouted Tag. 'Where did the vulture come from?'

More blue-white fire flashed off the crow as it morphed into an ancient woman, her long gray hair reaching to her knees, her back hunched with age, her face a network of lines and crevices. Only her eyes retained the fire of youth. And like the crow's they were completely black.

She stared at Tag and sneered. 'Vulture? Kiss me backside you chupid quashie. Fyah fi yuh. I's a Crow you mowly eediat.'

Tag's mouth dropped open as he found himself being roundly put down in perfect Jamaican patois. 'Sorry, everyting cook and curry, mama. You'se a crow, I believe.'

The Morrigan nodded her approval and then turned to face both William and Sylvian. 'Wolfman,' she greeted. 'Bloodborn. It's been a while.'

'Not long enough,' returned William. 'What do you want Morgan, or is it the Morrigan now?'

'Whatever you would like to use,' the goddess answered. 'I come as a friend, not a foe. The darkness approaches and I have come to assist in whatever way I might.'

'The cost of your assistance is oft too expensive,' interjected Sylvian. 'Ask Arthur or Lancelot. No,' he continued. 'You are not welcome here, goddess of battle. We can do without your…assistance.'

'Wait,' said the Morrigan. 'I have good news.' She turned to face Emily. 'Come to me, child.'

Em glanced at William who nodded slightly. Then she approached the bent crone and stood in front of her.

The Morrigan reached out, touched Emily on the cheek and smiled. 'Such power,' she said, her voice almost a whisper. 'Raw and untapped but I have not felt such power since the days of the round table. Good, you will need it,' she continued. 'And even with the wealth of power you have, it may not be enough. Anyhow, girl, your master, Merlin, he is alive.'

Emily frowned. 'Who?'

The Morrigan raised an eyebrow. 'Merlin Ambros Caledonensis Aurelius Ambrosius. The mage. Leader of the Shadowhunters.'

Emily looked blank for a few seconds then she finally asked again. 'Merlin?'

'Merlin Ambros,' explained Bastian. 'We call him by his other name. He prefers not to be called Merlin anymore. He took over the leadership of the Olympus Foundation after King Arthur died.'

Emily didn't look any more enlightened than she had before Bastian's cryptic explanation.

'Merlin? King Arthur. When was

someone going to tell me all of this?'

The Morrigan shook her head. 'Doesn't this child know anything?' she questioned scornfully.

'Wait,' interjected William. 'I thought Merlin was dead. I thought that he died many years ago, after Camelot.'

'Oh no,' denied the Morrigan. 'He slept for many moons, recovering. Even as he does now. But never dead. Not Merlin.'

'I had no idea,' admitted William. 'I left after the battle of Camllan and never returned to the cause. To tell the truth, I had enough. And I assumed that our mission had been fulfilled.'

'As did I,' added Sylvian. 'I also left the fold, except that I continued to pursue vamps on a more personal basis. So, Merlin alive? That crafty old conjurer will never cease to amaze me.'

'So why else are you here, goddess?' enquired William. 'I have never known you to go out of your way to bring good tidings. There is always a sting in the Morrigan's tail.'

'True,' admitted the Morrigan. 'I am oft the bearer of bad tidings. But that is not because I revel in them, it is merely because I do not shy from my duties.'

'So, tell all,' prompted William.

'The forces of darkness rail against you,' said the Morrigan.

'No shit,' quipped Emily. 'Tell us something that we don't know.'

The Morrigan stared at Emily with contempt. 'You may have power, child,' she said. 'But the scale of what you do not know is so vast that if I had to tell you all, then we would be dust before I finished.'

Emily looked down. 'I'm sorry,' she said. 'That was uncalled for. We've had a rough week.'

The Morrigan nodded. 'So you have. But believe me, it shall only get worse.' She turned back to William. 'I have just seen Janus Augusta.'

Both William and Sylvian drew a sharp breath. 'I thought he was dead,' observed William.

'As did I,' admitted the Morrigan. 'But no such luck. However, it is worse. Not only is he alive, he is now the head of the Italian house of the *Nosferatu* and also the *Capo di tutt'i capi* of the

Federation.'

'*Merde,*' swore Sylvian.

'How did the two of you not know this?' asked the Morrigan.

'How did *you* not know?' countered William.

'He is meant to be the mortal enemy of the both of you. Surely you kept track of him?'

'Obviously not,' answered William. 'Like you, we thought he suffered the true death after the Battle of Camllan. Damn it, I personally saw Sir Tristan and Sir Lamorak skewer him with their broadswords.'

'But did you see him die?' questioned the Morrigan.

William shook his head. 'Arthur had just been grievously wounded by the vampires and all eyes were on him.'

The Morrigan looked at Sylvian.

He too shook his head. 'As you know, the sun was down, it was dark, and we were fighting by torchlight. Sir Bors de Ganis and I were busy rushing to King Arthur's aid. I saw nothing.'

'Well, he is still alive,' she reiterated. 'And is currently the most powerful dark being in the world, not counting the gods, obviously.'

'Talking of which,' said William. 'Any chance of help from that angle?'

The Morrigan shook her head. 'I tried but they are not interested.'

'Oh well, there's a surprise,' quipped Sylvian.

'They feel that you have let them down,' explained the Morrigan. 'Lost faith.'

'That's simply not true,' countered William.

'They mean humanity in general,' continued the Morrigan. 'Not you and Sylvian *per se*.'

'What gods?' asked Em. 'What are you guys talking about?'

'There,' said the Morrigan. 'A case in point. The child doesn't even know of the existence of the gods, let alone worship them.'

'You mean like Thor and Zeus and those dudes?' asked Em.

William shook his head. 'No. The Greek and Roman pantheon have long since abandoned humanity. When the Christian god became popular, the lack of tangible worship reduced the old gods. Eventually they simply went away. There are still traces of them around, but they are almost impossible to contact.'

'Then what gods are you talking about?' asked Emily.

'The Celtic gods, mainly,' continued William. 'You see, even though Christianity has been the predominant religion in the United Kingdom and Europe for centuries, many people still pay homage to the old ways. They worship the old gods of earth and field and water. Even if they aren't aware that they are doing so.'

'I don't get it,' admitted Em. 'How do you pay homage to something and not even know that you are doing it?'

'Much of the worship has lost its true meaning to the people that practice it,' explained William. 'But the mere fact that they still go through the motions imparts a form of worship and this is enough to keep the Celtic gods alive.'

'What motions?'

'Nailing a horseshoe above your doorway to keep out bad luck. Picking a four-leaf clover for good luck. Throwing spilt salt over your shoulder. Knocking on wood. All of these little things are parts of greater ceremonies long since forgotten. But they still have power. The power to call, to entreat and to acknowledge. Enough power to sustain.

'The point of fact is that you will receive no help from that quarter,' repeated the Morrigan. 'And you will receive no help from Merlin for many months still to come. He is recovering but he was as near to death as to have actually crossed over. It is a tribute to his enormous strength and magical powers that he is still with us.'

William took a deep breath. 'So, we're on our own,' he remarked. 'Us and the Yardies. Not the greatest force known to man.'

The Morrigan shook her head.

'What?' asked William. 'Don't tell me, goddess of battle. More bad news?'

'I am truly sorry,' she said. 'Your friends, the men of Jamaican extraction, they are all dead.'

Tag jumped to his feet. 'No way,

mama-crow,' he cried. 'What you mean, dead?'

'The vampires,' said the Morrigan. 'Yesterday they overwhelmed them. If it is any consolation, they died well, killing all of the vampires that came for them. However, no Yardies survived.'

Tag buried his head in his hands and Emily walked over to him and put her arm around his shoulders. She said nothing. There was nothing to say. So, she merely held him and shared his grief.

'It is time,' said the Morrigan to William. 'Enough lurking and hiding in the shadows, Sir William Townsend. Once more the war is upon you. Call on your allies. Gird your loins and fight the good fight.'

William shook his head. 'Not again. Times have changed. I am no longer that person.'

'You are,' insisted the Morrigan. 'Call them. You are their leader.'

'No,' refuted William. 'I am a lone wolf. I am no longer pack. They have gone their own way.'

'Call them,' repeated the Morrigan.

'They have their own Alpha,' said William. 'I am no longer their leader.'

'They have an Alpha,' agreed the Morrigan. 'But you are the Omega Wolf. You are the leader of leaders. Call and they will come. The game has been played out, Sir William. And this is the only move left to make. It is the only option left open to you. Bring them together once more.'

William stood still for a while, his breathing slow and steady. Finally, he spoke.

'You are right, Morrigan,' he admitted. 'I shall call on the packs.'

'Good,' she said. 'When?'

William looked at her and his eyes flashed with power.

'I have just done so,' he said. 'Now we wait.'

The Morrigan smiled in satisfaction. The look was incongruous on her aged and care-worn face. 'My work is done for now.' The air around her shimmered with blue-white light as she transformed back into a giant crow.

Then she cocked her head to one side, flapped her wings, and she was gone.

'William,' said Emily. 'What the hell is actually going on?'

'Yeah,' agreed Bastian. 'My sentiments exactly.

Tell us what's happening, Wolfman.'

'I have summoned The Pack,' answered William.

'The Pack?' questioned Em.

'The Werewolf pack,' explained Sylvian. 'He has called them. They are coming.'

'What for?' asked Emily.

William turned to face her, and his eyes glowed with power as he spoke.

'They come to serve,' he answered. 'They come to destroy. They come to die.'

A low growl escaped his throat. 'They come for war.'

THE END ...For now.

A Note from the Author

Well, that's it for now. Emily and the rest will be back in **book 2: WOLFMAN.** http://a.co/gF7l9dV

I know that it's a hassle, but could you please leave a short review on Amazon if you can. It really helps others decide on whether or not to buy the book. http://a.co/4hA0dan Here is the link to leave reviews.

Also – as always, if you'd like to have a chat – my email is **zuffs@sky.com** Message me and I'll get straight back to you.

Here is the first chapter of WOLFMAN …hope that it appeals!

Thanks again for all – Craig Zerf

Preview

Wolfman: Emily Shadowhunter, Book Two
Chapter 1

The patch on the back of his leather jacket was so faded that you could only make out the writing in full sunlight.

"Protectors MC."

He stood at the bar, drinking. The barman had left the bottle of Jack Daniels in front of him. It was simply too much effort to keep filling the man's shot glass every twenty seconds. So instead he concentrated on polishing his beer glasses with a cloth that seemed to be made up of grease and cotton in equal measures, and he left the man to serve himself.

There were only another eight of them in the room, all with the same patch. And they were the sort of men that fill space.

Not only by the dint of their physical size, which was impressive, but also because of their presence. One of them could fill a room. Nine of them would have made the super bowl seem crowded.

These were men with presence.

But, although the barman had never seen them before and despite the fact that a room full of nine long-haired, leather-clad, visibly scarred, well-hard bikers should have filled him with trepidation – he felt at ease. He could sense that these were men that reacted to violence, but they would never be the root cause.

So, he provided the drinks and polished the crockery and didn't mention the fact that smoking indoors was illegal. And anyway, he was thankful for their custom. His pub was situated on an old main road that used to boast traffic and a steady clientele but, since the council had built a bypass, the pub had suddenly found itself in the back of beyond with barely enough traffic to sustain it.

Then he heard the sound of more

motorbikes pulling up outside the pub. Big machines with solid throaty engines. Harleys.

The men in the bar went from sitting in a relaxed fashion to standing and alert in one flowing move.

The sound of the bikes stuttered to a halt as the engines were turned off and, seconds later, another group of men walked into the pub.

They were made from the same mould as the Protectors MC. Large, raw boned but incongruously graceful. Long hair, beards, leather, denim. The patches on their backs read, "Bad Moon MC".

And for the first time the barman noticed that everyone in the room had the same color eyes. He wondered why he hadn't seen that before. It was so obvious. So undeniably strange.

Pale yellow. With flecks of gold.

Perhaps they were all wearing contact lenses, he thought. Some sort of biker thing. But he knew that these were not the type of men that bothered with cosmetic enhancements. So, instead of dwelling on it he simply polished harder.

One of the newcomers walked up to the man at the bar. The tension was almost visible.

He held out his hand. 'Lucas Cain?' he asked.

The man nodded, took the proffered hand. Shook once.

'Well met,' continued the newcomer. 'I be Jack Wishbone. Alpha of Bad Moon.'

'So, you heard the call?' asked Lucas.

'I did,' admitted Jack. 'We all did.'

Lucas put his empty glass down. 'Well then,' he said. 'Let's go.'

As one, the men trooped out of the pub. They didn't look back. Nor did they bid farewell to the barman.

But when he looked down he saw that, next to the half-empty bottle of whisky, the biker had left a pile of notes. A small fortune. Enough to pay for a hundred bottles, let alone the half that he had consumed. He flicked through the notes, baffled at the bizarre display of generosity.

Outside the rumble of engines shook the ground as the combined crew set off.

And the barman, who had fought in both the Falklands and Iraq before he hung up his spurs, couldn't shake the powerful impression the group of men he had just seen were going to war. A war from which they did not all expect to come back from.

Made in the USA
Las Vegas, NV
10 September 2023

77407706R00187